A SIMPLE CHOICE

Kingsley Allen Whipple

authorHOUSE®

AuthorHouse™
1663 Liberty Drive
Bloomington, IN 47403
www.authorhouse.com
Phone: 1 (800) 839-8640

Published by AuthorHouse 03/16/2020

ISBN: 978-1-5462-2036-7 (sc)
ISBN: 978-1-5462-2035-0 (e)

Library of Congress Control Number: 2017918807

Print information available on the last page.

Any people depicted in stock imagery provided by Getty Images are models, and such images are being used for illustrative purposes only. Certain stock imagery © Getty Images.

This book is printed on acid-free paper.

Because of the dynamic nature of the Internet, any web addresses or links contained in this book may have changed since publication and may no longer be valid. The views expressed in this work are solely those of the author and do not necessarily reflect the views of the publisher, and the publisher hereby disclaims any responsibility for them.

to whom much is given...

Every so often, events will transpire which could have the potential to have a lasting and profound effect on the trajectory of one's life. More often than not, they tend to happen at the most inopportune of times. It all began with a 2 am call.

"I'm being pulled over," said the voice on the phone.

Before Josh could bring his mind into focus, the phone went silent. The number on the screen didn't trigger any connections...

Adam and Clare made their way down the corridor of the old Victorian home towards the only room that showed any signs of life. The young couple moved toward the dim, yellowish light, which spilled into the otherwise dark and musty hallway. To say that they were conservatively dressed qualifies as an abuse of the term understatement. The only missing garment

1

from his ensemble would have been a neatly folded, chickadee colored sweater draped upon his shoulders to complement his tan khakis and well-worn penny loafers.

Theirs was a truly match made in heaven. Aside from being devoutly religious, everything they did seemed to announce to the world that they would never think about deviating from their chosen path. Their mannerisms seemed to mirror one another, so much so, that they often finished each other's sentences.

Clare Robinson, right down to her choice of shoes, was the embodiment of sensible. Her dirty blond hair which she had pulled back neatly into a simple, twisted, topknot bun announced to the world that she wouldn't be wasting any of her precious time fiddling with lose strands. She unequivocally understood how the world should work and she knew her exact place in it.

A stack of paperwork appeared to be trying to do its best to conceal an oversized mahogany desk. Behind a mountain of files, they could hear one-half of what they could only assume to be a rather intriguing conversation.

"Take a deep breath, I need you to think about the big picture," Josh said. "Now is not the time to go into panic mode. I understand things seem a bit overwhelming

Paco, but when all is said and done, hopefully this will seem like nothing more than a minor speed bump."

"Let me make sure I've got all the details straight. You were pulled over last night for what the police said was an illegal lane change?"

Adam sheepishly knocked in such a delicate fashion as if not to disturb any sleeping mice, which might possibly be within earshot.

A hand appeared from behind the heaping pile and encouraged the doorknockers in. The couple neatly folded themselves into the chairs facing his desk. With the phone cradled in his ear, peaking thru the clutter he pointed to the ceiling and continued his conversation.

"Upon searching your car they found 16 packets of heroin totaling approximately 26 grams. You said it was in the glove box?"

Adam and Clare looked at each other with an equal combination of curious amazement and utter disgust.

"Did they find anything else in the car? No guns, no weed, no open containers?"

He appeared to be scribbling in some sort of ancient Sanskrit on a yellow legal pad.

"Were you drinking?"

"How much?"

"Seriously?"

"Did you make a statement? Well, thank God for small miracles, I'm glad you remembered."

"It's going to be okay. Was there anyone else in the car?"

"Was she arrested as well?"

"No, that shouldn't be a problem. I know that from where you are sitting this might not make sense to you, but I want you to keep an open mind. In the grand scheme of things Paco, this might turn out to be a blessing is disguise."

"I've been doing this for almost twenty years. I'm speaking from experience, that's how."

"Unfortunately, I can't do this without your help. Despite the fact that we live in a world of instant gratification, I'm pleading with you to exercise a little patience. The arraignment is set for Monday morning. Once we get you out on bail, we'll have more time to go over all the details. No, that's enough for now; I will get the rest then."

"One more thing ... did you call your dad?"

Josh exhaled a heavy sigh. "I understand... You do know your dad loves you – right?"

"And you know that there is nothing you could do that would change that ... right?"

"Paco, I'm not going to try and tell you what to do; I understand it's your choice."

"Look, I realize that it's easier said than done, but you're going to have to try and relax."

"I didn't say that. It's really no big deal. The truth is that I'd only be pretending to love you if I wasn't willing to sacrifice a little bit of my time to help you out. I'm asking you to trust me. I want you to know that in the end, everything is going to work out fine."

"No, no... there's really no need to apologize."

"We can't get you in front of a judge until Monday. Are you going to be okay 'til then?"

"Are you sure?"

"I'll see you on Monday."

"Don't worry, I know where."

"Love you too little buddy."

Josh shifted his attention to the couple seated before him. "I'm sorry, may I help you?"

"Please forgive the intrusion," Adam implored. "Since your office was the only one showing any signs of life, we were hoping you might be able to point us in the right direction. We're looking for Mr. Joshua Randall."

"You're looking at him."

Joshua Randall was a serial juggler. Since graduating Law School, he understood that in order to get ahead in his chosen specialty, it would require having multiple clients at all times. What he lacked in billable hourly income, he more than made up in sheer volume.

They stared at him in disbelief. Their ever so slight discomfort, instantaneously evaporated into warm smiles.

"I'm sorry Mr. Randall we are the Robinsons," said Adam. "Hopefully my cousin, William told you we were coming."

Momentarily puzzled, Josh snapped his fingers in quick succession as if trying to awaken a long-forgotten memory. "That's right," wagging his finger. "You guys are the pastry makers."

"Exactly," Adam confirmed. "We are the owners of Heavenly Treats in Lakewood."

Josh extended his hand.

"I'm Adam, and this is my wife Clare."

"Pleasure to meet you," as Josh exchanged handshakes. "What can I do for you?"

"Forgive me for being so forward," Adam cautiously interjected. "But there must be some confusion... we were told you handled constitutional law not criminal law."

"Who said that?"

"My cousin informed me ..." Adam started to say.

Josh held up his hand and stopped him mid-sentence.

"I never tried to imply that I was anything but a criminal attorney." Josh thought about it for a moment and helpfully added, "Sorry for the misunderstanding, these days it's mostly criminal law but I did specialize in Constitutional law way back in law school."

Josh noticed both Adam and Clare gaze subtlety upward over his left shoulder towards his law degree, which, in fact, did confirm that he had graduated from University of Michigan.

"I'm sorry to take up your time Mr. Randall but this isn't a criminal matter," said Adam in a most apologetic tone.

"That's okay," Josh acknowledged. "I was the one who told Bill that I would be happy to help if I could. Are you guys hungry?"

"Excuse me?" Adam said in a quizzical tone.

"You do eat ... don't you?"

"Of course, we eat Mr. Randall." Clare chimed in, "but this is extremely important to us."

"Josh, please" he said with a heavy sigh, "and I am fairly certain that I have the mental capacity to be able to listen to your story while simultaneously eating."

"It is just that we were actually hoping to get the ball rolling on this," exclaimed Adam.

"I totally understand," Josh replied. "But it's been a very long day and I am starving. Come on, I know a great little place right around the corner."

"We weren't..." Clare tried to interject.

"Don't worry," Josh responded.

Trying to be as polite as possible, Adam meekly replied. "Perhaps we caught you at a bad time.... maybe..."

"Nonsense," Josh interrupted, "we can talk on the way."

do not be afraid

They covered the three and a half blocks it had taken them to traverse from Josh's office to the restaurant in a blur of informal chitchat covering a plethora of topics from the inconsistencies in the weather all the way up to the lack of intriguing movies worth seeing these days. Upon entering, Clare immediately noticed that the dining establishment Josh had chosen was a lot closer to a bar than an actual restaurant. The clientele was a smorgasbord of young professionals, college students, and bohemian hippies with a heavy emphasis on the later.

The hostess recognized Josh immediately and ushered the patrons to a high-top table located in the bar section of the restaurant.

"Afternoon Josh," said the bubbly young teenager. "I think Julie is going to be your server today. Can I take your drink order while you are waiting?"

Swaying his open palm, Josh gestured for Adam and Clare to order first.

"Do you have any ginger ale?" Clare inquired.

"I think we might be able to scrounge some up," the hostess cheerfully replied. "And for you?" looking at Adam.

"Water will be just fine," said Adam.

The hostess turned her attention back to Josh "Are we sticking with Coors Light today?"

"Works for me."

Clare gave her husband's hand a little extra squeeze.

"I take it you are not particularly happy with my choice of venues?" Josh asked, with a friendly smile.

"No," Clare lied, while trying her very best to conceal her displeasure.

"I happen to like colorful people." Josh playfully divulged.

"I'm sure the food will be fine," Adam cautiously interjected. "It is just that we usually don't spend much time in bars that's all."

They proceeded with the usual pleasantries of getting to know one another all the way up until the waitress had finished taking their order.

The front door opened and a cloud of marijuana smoke seeped into the room. A young couple in dreadlocks was trying to squeeze their way past Clare towards the bar. Meanwhile, Clare was doing her best to try and shrink herself into her chair as if for fear that the new arrivals might possibly be carrying a hereto-unknown strain of toxic syphilis.

"I take it you disapprove," Josh noted.

"Do not be deceived Mr. Randall, bad company corrupts good morals," Clare happily pointed out.

Josh tilted his head slightly "You like to judge don't you Mrs. Robinson?"

Adam glanced over at his wife and noticed that she looked as though she was secretly trying to chew off an imaginary canker sore from the inside of her cheek.

"Excuse me?" Clare said, with all the righteous indignation she could muster.

"I'm sorry: I didn't realize I was stuttering. I said you like to judge, don't you?" Josh repeated.

"How could you say such a thing?" Adam demanded, as if to protect her honor.

"Somehow I get the feeling that you seem to have the notion that you are morally superior to all these people in here." Josh exclaimed, as he waved his hand in an open gesture. "You know absolutely nothing about them and yet, here you sit on your high throne ready to judge them. The sad part is that it seems like you've already made up your mind that these are bad people."

"I certainly have not," said Clare trying her best to convince herself that he was wrong.

"While I am one hundred percent certain that there are some truly bad people in this world," Josh continued, "I would like to believe that for the most part, people are basically good and they are actually trying their best to be decent, honest and kind to others. They are just trying to get through the day to day bullshit that goes on in this life."

Clare winced upon hearing him cuss, as if simply being associated with such a vulgarian might condemn her soul to the very depths of hell.

It's no wonder why Christianity is on the decline, Josh thought to himself. He decided to soften his tone and to placate his potential clients he added, "You needn't get so defensive; people judge...it's what we do. For all I know, you could be judging me right now. I suppose that it is possible that even as you are sitting here, you could be contemplating whether or not you think this is going to be worth your time."

From the death grip Clare gave Adam's hand beneath the table, he understood she wanted to flee from Josh's presence as if Satan, himself were sitting before them.

"I believe we are called to live Godly lives Mr. Randall." Clare said, as she regained her composure.

Josh's eyes softened. "I'm sorry it has been a really long day and I wasn't trying to offend you. Please forgive me."

Clare slowly unclenched her hand and the blood gradually returned to her husband's tortured fingers.

"Its okay, Mr. Randall." Adam jumped in, hoping to save his wife from further discomfort. "Perhaps this wasn't such a good idea. I'm just not so sure you might be the best fit. No offense, but we were really hoping to work with a Christian lawyer that's all."

"What makes you think that I'm not a Christian?" Josh politely asked, then turning on a dime, he smugly added... "Would you have felt more convinced had there been a giant crucifix hanging on my office wall?"

"I really don't appreciate your tone Mr. Randall; it is not only condescending, but dripping with sarcasm." Clare said, with all the authority of one who truly knows the subtleties of the English language.

Just as in a cheesy Hollywood movie when the cavalry arrives in the nick of time: a friendly teenage waitress arrived with a steaming hot pepperoni pizza. As she placed it in the center of the table, she was more than happy to disclose the obvious. "Careful it's hot."

"If you are looking for perfection, you're not going to find it here. Sadly, I don't always choose the right words. There may even be times when it seems like I might be pushing your buttons," Josh bluntly pointed out, then softened his tone. "I will apologize in advance if I slip up, because it's really not my intention to attack your faith."

"It's not a very becoming quality Mr. Randall," Clare proclaimed.

"You are probably right." Although a bit weak, it was the best excuse Josh could come up with at the moment. "Look, you guys came all the way down here; let's see what we can do to move things in the right direction. Bill gave me a condensed version of the events that happened but I think it would probably be best if you start from the beginning."

Clare glimpsed over at her husband for some sign of approval: with his encouraging nod she gave a heavy sigh and trudged right in.

"The details are a bit hazy," said Clare, "because it didn't seem all that important at the time".

'It seemed like just another day, "Adam chirped in, trying his best to be helpful.

"I remember hearing the sleigh bells affixed to the door indicating yet another customer. His demeanor seemed pleasant enough," she politely recounted.

"When he said he'd like to order a wedding cake, our immediate reaction was of course. Since we weren't that busy, I actually ushered him into the back room to sit down so we could look through pictures of different wedding cakes that we make. Perhaps he had mentioned that this was going to be for a gay wedding right from the very beginning, but it wasn't until a few minutes later when he started talking about his partner, that it finally sank in."

Clare continued with her story. "It was at this point that I politely informed him that we were Christians and we really didn't feel comfortable making a cake for a gay wedding. I even suggested a few other bakeries that I thought would be happy to accommodate him."

"Was he upset?" Josh asked, trying to gather as much information as possible.

"In all actuality, he didn't seem offended. He even opened up about how his parents were Lutherans and they were still a bit uncomfortable with the idea. I still don't know why he changed his mind." Clare wondered aloud.

the blind leading the blind

It was one of those perfect, cloudless, Sunday mornings where the temperature was already creeping up towards the mid-sixties before 9 am. The outdoor patio provided a panoramic view of not only the town below, but the entire metro area stretching towards the eastern horizon. Thomas and Jeremy were sipping mimosas from elegant, baccarat champagne flutes while Ethan was patiently waiting for his turn so that he could give his name to the hostess for the next available table.

Thomas and Ethan had been together for almost six years now, ever since meeting backstage at the Guys and Dolls production at the Performing Arts Center. Once the state of Colorado announced that they would be legalizing gay marriage, they immediately went down to the courthouse. However, after much deliberation they opted for a much more traditional ceremony.

"How are the wedding plans coming along Thomas?" Jeremy inquired.

"Swimmingly, everything is finally coming together as planned. You did receive your invitation, didn't you?" Thomas Addicott said with a smile.

"What, you didn't get my RSVP?" Jeremy asked in a slightly alarmed tone.

"That's Ethan's department," Thomas reminded him.

"I should have known."

"We had a little bit of a hiccup with the wedding cake though," Thomas volunteered. "Our first choice wasn't able to accommodate us so we ending up going with Sweet Cakes over on Broadway."

"Oh, I love that shop, they make the best cannolis," said Jeremy reminiscing about their yumminess.

"To die for," Thomas agreed.

Between sips of mimosa Jeremy asked, "I'm a little bit curious, why were they your second choice?"

"Nothing really, Ethan and I really liked this one shop over there on Colfax but the owners at Heavenly Treats didn't feel comfortable baking a wedding cake for us."

"I'm so sorry," Jeremy offered sympathetically.

"About what?"

"How bigoted some people can be."

"Jeremy, I think you're wrong. Actually, they were quite nice about it. She simply said that because of their religious beliefs, they wouldn't feel comfortable making the cake for our wedding she even went so far as to give me several local bakeries that she thought would be able to accommodate us. She was actually the one who called Sweet Cakes and set up the appointment for us."

Sensing an opportunity, Jeremy completely ignored the last statement. "I know that with the wedding and everything else going on, you and Ethan have a lot on your plate but I will happily take on this case for you. They most definitely violated your civil rights."

Although Jeremy Mendoza was a corporate attorney by trait, he had been doing pro bono work for the Colorado chapter of the A.C.L.U. since 1989. Everything about him reeked of success. His immaculately manicured nails were more than likely, the envy of many women. Aside from living a comfortable lifestyle, which he clearly enjoyed, Jeremy was fascinated by the law.

"What do you mean case? Violated my civil rights?"

"The law is very clear on this," Jeremy divulged. "State law prohibits public accommodations including businesses from refusing service based on factors such as race, sex, marital status or sexual orientation."

"But they didn't..."

Jeremy cut him off mid-sentence. "This kind of bigotry is disgusting and we need to put a stop to it. I am so sick and tired of religious zealots thinking that they are so morally superior. I am dumbfounded as to how some people can be so narrow-minded. Treating gay people differently because of who we are is discrimination, plain and simple. A tolerant and free society has no room for bigots."

With the money this case would potentially bring him, Jeremy could practically smell the plush, full grain leather seats on the new Range Rover that he had been ogling last week. "You deserve to be compensated," he added greedily.

"This isn't about money," Thomas initially claimed, but was now starting to feel as though somehow, he might have been slighted.

"Of course not, it's about your human dignity. What this lawsuit says is that we will not tolerate being treated as second-class citizens because of our sexual orientation. The law is clearly on our side. Somebody has to take a stand. I'm so sick and tired of peoplee trying to hide behind religion as an excuse for their bigotry."

"They really didn't seem like bigots." Thomas said defensively, as he reflected upon the meeting.

'"That's the most devious part." Jeremy rationalized. "They act as though they really care about you right up until the very moment, they find out you don't subscribe to their beliefs."

the letter of the law

"So was he mad when he left?" Josh asked with all sincerity.

"I don't think so," Clare said. "He actually bought some tea cakes before leaving."

"Hmmph!" Josh added thoughtfully.

"Does that mean anything to you?" Adam said, hoping to inject himself back into the conversation.

"Maybe he likes tea cakes." Josh replied in a playful manner. "I've got some good news and bad news."

"Might as well give us the bad news first," Clare politely offered up.

"In the state of Colorado, there does not need to be a unanimous decision in order to side with the plaintiff. There only needs to be a simple majority."

"What does that mean?" Adam inquired.

Sensing that he was already skating on thin ice, Josh wisely resisted the temptation to sarcastically explain the definition of majority.

"It simply means that here in Colorado, in a civil lawsuit the plaintiffs don't need a unanimous decision in order to win; they only need to convince seven people out of twelve people on the jury that you violated their client's civil rights."

"But you had mentioned there was some good news?"

"The good news is that Constitutionally, I think that you really do have a pretty good case. The first amendment states that Congress shall make no law respecting an establishment of religion, or prohibiting the free exercise thereof; it is the free exercise part that we will be concentrating on." Josh continued, "According to the summons, the lawsuit brought on by the plaintiffs states they are seeking three hundred and fifty thousand dollars in punitive damages because of your refusal to bake their wedding cake."

"The reality is that we are faced with a set of conflicting laws. On the one hand, you have the first amendment which guarantees that Congress shall make no law impeding the free exercise of religion, and then on the opposing side you have the civil right act of 1964 which outlawed discrimination on the basis of race, color, religion, sex, or national origin and was later amended to include sexual orientation."

"And you call this good news?" Adam interjected.

Holding up his hand, "I wasn't quite finished yet" Josh continued. "The problem we are facing is that we have two valid laws which seemingly oppose each other. The basis of your defense relies upon the first amendment, which guarantees you the right to worship your God as you see fit. And as such, you feel that being forced to bake a cake for a gay wedding would go against your biblical beliefs."

"Exactly," declared Adam.

"But right now, the law is clearly on our side." Clare asserted.

"It is a little bit trickier than that. Actually, you both have legitimate arguments. The reason why I believe you will prevail is because the first amendment should take precedence. One could easily argue that this is a very slippery slope. If the courts were to side with the plaintiffs, they would be opening themselves up to a whole new can of worms. Think about it... imagine if someone went into a Muslim printing shop and demanded that they print cartoons depicting their prophet performing lewd sexual acts with a camel. Just the mere suggestion of such a disgusting thing would garner a death sentence in many Islamic countries. Thankfully, I believe no responsible judge would allow that to happen."

"The way I understand it," Josh continued "if the law is to mean anything at all, you should be free to worship your God any way you like. This means that you should not be forced to do anything which violates your religious principles."

"So, you think that we were within our legal rights?" Clare hinted, hoping for confirmation.

"I think that we have a really good case" Josh said between bites of pizza. "It may take going all the way to the Supreme Court to decide but I think the law is clearly on our side."

"This means that we are going to win, right?" Adam speculated, itching to hear only good news.

"Not so fast, I said I believe we have an excellent case, but that doesn't mean the court will necessarily be sympathetic to our plight."

"How can that be?" Clare asked, while wondering if she had missed something.

"I'm not sure if you have noticed, despite what our founding fathers may have intended: we have been moving steadily towards a more secular society."

"Oh, we are well aware," Adam vocalized in a tone of almost complete disgust.

"If surveys are to be believed," Josh explained, "odds are that not everyone on that jury will believe in God, or at least the same God."

Adam could see that Clare was equally as confused with that last part of the statement.

"From the way you are talking," said Clare, "it seems like you are open to helping us. Does that mean you are willing to take the case Mr. Randall?"

"More importantly, how much is this going to cost us?" Adam asked, hoping that it didn't sound too greedy.

"We really don't have a lot of money," Clare volunteered.

"I am willing to take it pro bono on one condition," Josh offered, "I am going to have to insist that we do this my way."

"We really appreciate your generous offer to take this case pro bono Mr. Randall, but that doesn't give you the right to dictate the terms." Adam said, defiantly.

"No, I'm sorry, that's exactly what it means. It means that I am donating my time for free to help you. I totally understand if you wish to find someone else. Actually, I can respect that."

"I'm not trying to fight you on this," Josh continued, "but I am very good at what I do just as I am sure that you are good at what you do. Imagine if I were to go into your bakery and tell you how you should make your cupcakes, I suspect that wouldn't go over so well."

Adam and Clare exchanged glances as if they were simultaneously realizing they were about to make a huge mistake.

"This is not open for discussion," Josh insisted. "If you want to proceed, I will need you to come by my office Monday afternoon. I feel obligated to warn you though, I can't promise you that this will be the easiest task you will ever undertake. You might even find this kind of painful, because your beliefs are going to be challenged every step of the way. If you have any reservations at all; now is the time to walk away. Once you go so far down the rabbit hole, there isn't going to be any way you can put the genie back in the bottle."

Clare seemed a little confused by his use of mixed metaphors. She wasn't sure if she should run away in horror or soldier on but for some inexplicable reason a random thought came to mind and she found herself smiling. Yes, He does, she thought to herself, the Lord does work in mysterious ways.

meditate day and night

Large splatters began randomly appearing on the windshield of their Volvo. Adam switched on the wipers which made quick work of the annoying drops.

"I really don't like him," Clare blurted out as if she had been holding her breath since they parted ways. "I think he is rude, condescending and arrogant."

"I'm not saying he is a perfect match."

"Perfect?" Clare responded with utter amazement. "He was already reaching for a slice of pizza before we had time to even *think* about saying grace."

"I know," Adam said in a soothing voice. "But he seems to know the law and he agreed to take the case pro bono. At this point, I really don't know what other options we have."

"We could choose to defend ourselves you know, after all we do have God on our side."

They both lovingly smiled at one another, as if sharing a private inside joke.

"As tempting as that may sound," Adam said, "I still think we would be much better off having a skilled attorney arguing on our behalf."

Clare's eyes softened, "There is something about him I can't quite put my finger on but if you are okay with this, so am I."

"We'll pray on it," Adam proclaimed.

Clare smiled and breathed a heavy sigh as she lovingly caressed his hand.

the writing on the wall

Josh arrived at the courtroom with just a few minutes to spare. Thank goodness the assistant D.A., Rebecca Dimitri, was handling the case. She definitely had a soft spot for first time offenders. Josh approached her table and she clinically gave him all the details.

The bailiff ushered six scruffy looking men of various shapes and ages all handcuffed and wearing identical construction-cone orange colored jump suits.

Paco, a.k.a. Francisco Dominguez was a scrappy young man. His youthful appearance and small frame betrayed the fact that he was almost nineteen years old. His wanna be stash neither made him look any older or tougher than he would have liked. Moderation was not an adjective that came to mind if his friends were to describe him. Paco enjoyed drugs, plain and simple and if there was a party to be found, he was always the instigator trying to ratchet it up to the next level. From his worldview, life was one giant party and he was determined not to miss out on any of it. Despite usually being one of the smartest people in the room, it didn't always help him make the right decisions.

Paco was last in the line of shackled prisoners, and his eyes scanned the courtroom for a friendly face. His mood lightened when he spotted Josh leaning over and talking to a very pretty woman who was probably still in her late twenties sitting at what appeared to be the prosecutioner's desk.

Josh walked over to the bench where Paco was sitting and took the seat next to him.

"Thanks for coming to the rescue."

"Don't worry about it. I don't have a lot of time to talk right now," Josh whispered, "but when they call your case, I'm going to need you to stand - look directly at the judge and be as polite as possible. After they read the charges, the judge will ask you how you would like to plead. I just want you to say not guilty your honor... nothing more, understood?"

"Understood."

When the clerk announced the first case on the docket number zero two one, zero one nine, six four State of Colorado vs. Francisco Dominguez, Paco stood and faced the judge.

Ms. Dimitri told the court in a detached manner that the defendant was apprehended on the 17th of May 2016.

"The defendant is charged with driving under the influence and possession with intent to deliver of a Schedule 1 controlled substance. The penalty for which, carries a sentence of up to no more than five year's incarceration in a state penitentiary and / or a fine of no more than ten thousand dollars. Do you understand these charges?"

Paco nodded his head and said yes.

"And do you wish to enter a plea?"

"Not guilty your honor."

Rebecca chimed in "Normally for a crime of this magnitude, bail would usually be set at $10,000 but since the defendant has no criminal history, the state is willing to lower the bail to $1,000."

"Does the defense have any objections?" The judge officially asked.

"No objections your honor." Josh said, as he rose slightly from his seat.

"So be it, bail is set at $1,000."

The judge looked down at his calendar and said, "Preliminary trial next week on the 28th does that work for everyone?"

Josh stood and addressed the bench. "Your honor, at this time we would like to request the preliminary hearing be pushed back until after June 21st." Josh added, "My client will need the additional time in which to complete a thirty-day treatment in rehabilitation."

Paco did a double-take and stared at Josh in disbelief. Deep down inside he was seething. He couldn't believe what he was hearing, Josh was supposed to be his friend. How could he possibly be betraying him like this?

actions speak louder than words

Josh stood as he heard the steel door opening. It was good to see Paco uncuffed and back in street clothes. He was happy to see that he was wearing a flannel instead of his customary wife beater, sleeveless tee shirt that accentuated his somewhat scrawny, tatted arms.

The forty-five minutes it had taken to process the paperwork had given Paco sufficient time to cool down and he reluctantly greeted him with a hug. As thankful as he was to be free, thirty days in rehab was not exactly what he had planned upon his release.

As they were walking across the parking lot, before Paco had a chance to talk, Josh started the conversation.

"What the hell were you thinkin?" Josh demanded in a tone that meant business.

"I'm sorry Josh, I screwed up."

"Ya think? I get it, you might be a little pissed about the rehab but hear me out first, and then you can say your piece. Okay?"

"Okay."

"This isn't my first rodeo Paco. The drunk driving charge isn't going to go away. There is zero chance I can get that one dropped. No matter what, you're going to have a mandatory 40 hours of drug and alcohol classes and up to 96 hours of community service. The drug and alcohol classes you can bang out while you are at rehab. I think I might be able to pull some strings so you can complete your community service there as well."

Josh continued, "As far as the drug charges, you said the stuff was in the glove compartment, right?"

"Yeah."

"You're not lying to me Paco, are you?"

"Nope, it was in an envelope in the glove box. They must have found it when they were searching the car while I was sitting in the back of the cruiser."

"Well that's good news."

"How's that good news?"

"Because they didn't have a warrant to search your car, I'm fairly confident that we can get those charges tossed."

"Then why the hell am I going to rehab if I only have to worry about a stupid drunk driving?"

"You don't get it Paco, there are no guarantees in this life. I can't possibly know exactly what what's going to happen. The best advice I can give you is to prepare for the worst possible outcome. Anything after that is gravy."

"But why…"

Josh cut him off midsentence. "Paco, I'm not going to argue with you on this one. As much as you want to say you don't have a problem, if you want my help, this is the way it is going to have to be. Comprende?"

"Comprende." Paco responded in the usual gringo fashion.

"How much?" Josh pleaded.

"What do you mean?"

"Don't act stupid, I'm not as dumb as I look."

"A couple of times a week at the most," Paco tried to assure him.

Josh knew it was a lie but he didn't press it. No one ever thinks about selling heroin if they are still spending less than a hundred dollars a week on their habit.

"How are you holding up now?"

"I'm fine, I know what I am doing. I've got things under control."

"I can see that." Josh sarcastically replied.

"You want to put this behind you …right? I can assure you that everything will go much more smoothly, once you are all polished up. After you've completed rehab and you can stand before the judge and say with all honesty, that you have been drug and alcohol free for the past thirty days it going to go a long, long way."

Paco tried to protest but before he could articulate a good argument, Josh continued.

"I suspect that you might be tempted to claim that the reason why you like doing drugs is because you think that they make you feel good. I would venture to say that there is an entirely different reason."

"Huh?"

"Although this might not make sense to you right now, I believe that what you are sub-consciously trying to do is search for a deeper meaning to life. If you are being completely honest with yourself, I think everybody feels like an outsider at one point or another. From the time we are born I think each and every one of us instinctively knows that there is something missing. More often than not, we will do whatever we can to try and fill that void. Some people use drugs, some alcohol, some sex… I think we are all guilty of using distractions to combat this emptiness, it is just that some of the choices we make are more destructive than others."

"What are you talking about?"

"It's not my intention to get all philosophical on you right now. For the time being, I think it is far more important to concentrate on helping you get sober. Before you get all nervous, I'm not trying to insinuate that you can never drink again. Hopefully, a month of sobriety will help you understand that doing drugs and being drunk all the time isn't a very healthy career choice. Sometimes life can spiral out of control. One bad mistake can lead to another and before you know it you've gone so far down a path it seems like it is the only possible road. I am telling you right now, it is never too late to change." Josh continued, "You're a smart kid, I know you can do this standing on your head. When it's all over and done with and you can put this mess behind you – then you get to choose the direction you want your life to take."

As they walked thru the parking lot towards Josh's car, Paco reluctantly resigned himself to his fate.

"If I'm going to do this, you're gonna have to swing by the 7-11, I need to get some smokes, there is no way I'm going to get thru rehab without em."

"You're not smoking in my car."

"It's a friggin convertible."

"Doesn't matter, you're still not smoking in my car."

As soon as Paco walked out of the store, he immediately tore into the carton and lit up a Marlboro.

Josh patiently waited for him to finish his cigarette before they started the trek. The first couple of miles Josh drove in silence giving him ample time to think about his predicament, then Josh decided to delve a little deeper...

"Paco," Josh said, in a loving tone.

"Yeah?"

"I thought you were smarter than that?"

"Me too. I know, it probably wasn't one of my better choices."

"Yup. It's okay, we all make mistakes: it comes with the territory. You do realize that at some point you're going to have to call your dad."

"I know, but you won't rat me out … will you?"

"No Paco, I won't rat you out, but I won't lie for you either. You've got to do it soon. Believe me; a call coming from you after you have voluntarily checked yourself into rehab won't be nearly as bad as if he finds out what happened on his own."

"I know you're right. I'll call him soon," Paco said with a heavy sigh… "Promise."

"Please do. You do know your dad loves you … right?" Josh reminded him.

"I suppose."

"And you know that there is nothing you can ever do that would change how he feels about you?"

"If you say so."

"I do. Try not to worry Paco, things will get better. I'll track down your car and get it out of hock…not that you'll be needing it soon." Josh added in a teasing manner.

"Thanks for not rubbing it in."

"It's the least I could do under the circumstances."

As Josh drove in silence, Paco quietly brooded about his predicament. It didn't make any sense. How could the cop have possibly known to look in the glove box? Who would ever think of opening up a sealed, bulk-mail offer from a credit card company?

Paco replayed the events in his mind...he was certain that there was still a stack of unopened mail from his P.O. Box.

He knew that even if someone were to examine the envelope, there was no way of telling that it had been steamed open. He was positive that he tossed the glue stick underneath his driver's seat just so as not to arouse suspicion. It had to be a set-up, he thought to himself. The only person who he had ever told about his envelope trick was his connection Skeeter.

Paco had never even given it a second thought when Skeeter asked him why he insisted on using seals instead of balloons. The more Paco thought about it, the more his blood began to boil.

"I'm going to kill him." Paco half-muttered under his breath.

Paco's barely audible outburst jarred Josh out of his own thought process. "What the hell are you mumbling about?"

"I was set up. That piece of sh** was either a narc or he's working with the cops. If I ever see that jerk again, I'm going to kill him."

Josh gave a quick glance in his rearview to make sure the coast was clear and jammed on his brakes as hard as he could.

"What the ..." Paco blurted out, as his head lurched toward the dash before the seatbelt reigned him in.

"Have I got your attention now?" Josh demanded.

Paco jerked his head around and looked at Josh in astonishment.

"What the hell is wrong with you?" Josh challenged. "You just got popped with enough smack to put you away for half a dozen years and now all of a sudden you think you're a tough guy?"

"Relax, I'm just venting," Paco lied, secretly hoping that this answer would pacify him.

"You really don't get it, do you? Paco, this isn't a joke. Let's say you are right and you were set up. You really think killing an undercover cop is somehow going to make your life any better? Getting revenge is not the answer. It's poison and it will ruin your life. You've gotta let it go. I don't mean to get all biblical on you, but sometimes there is no other way."

On a certain level Paco knew Josh was right, but all he could think about was getting even. However, he wisely decided to keep his thoughts to himself. They drove the remaining few miles towards the foothills in silence.

As they pulled into the long, winding driveway towards First Step, Josh started the conversation back up. "I realize that at the present moment you might find this situation to be a little intimidating because you are facing the unknown. I am asking you to exercise a little faith. I'm sure that there are probably a million other things you'd rather be doing but I'm urging you to please see this all the way through."

I'd rather stick a fork in my eye; Paco thought to himself, but said nothing.

"Look around you, there are no fences, no armed guards. No one is putting a gun to your head and forcing you to do this. I'm asking you to stick it out because I love you and I don't want to see you flush your future down the toilet. Not for my sake, but for yours. I'm not going to promise you that this will be all sunshine and lollipops but I'm hoping that you won't quit halfway into it. Perhaps once you realize that they have your best interests at heart, it might help you understand that you are headed down a dead-end road and ultimately you need to change directions."

"I get it, you are here under duress. The way I see it, you can either just go through the motions or you can actually make the most of the situation."

"How could I possibly make the most of the situation?"

"I've never been to rehab myself," Josh admitted. "But I suspect you are probably going to have to sit through a bunch of counseling sessions, just be open to what you are hearing."

"Why?"

"Well, I'm hoping that once you start paying attention, perhaps it might give you a whole new perspective on life.

"Fat chance of that," Paco blurted out.

"This isn't a joke Paco," Josh reminded him. "I'm asking you to please take this seriously. I hate to burst your bubble, but life is all about making choices, some good some bad. The better your choices, the better your future. Although this may seem a bit confusing to you now, I am cautiously optimistic that at some point this will eventually start to make sense."

When they pulled up to the door Josh assured him, "Everything has already been taken care of; all you need to do is check yourself in."

"Aren't you coming?"

"This one's all on you pal. I'll be back to check in on you later but this is something you need to do on your own."

"Thanks," Paco said somewhat begrudgingly.

"Hey Paco,"

"Yeah?"

"Try not to look so glum, things will get better."

"I suppose," Paco tried his best to convince himself; as he turned and walked inside.

on rocky ground

As Josh was walking down the hallway, he spotted Clare and Adam sitting directly across from the receptionist's desk. "Glad to see you guys decided to proceed."

"You seem a bit surprised," Clare responded.

"Sometimes I tend to be brutally honest," Josh said, as he encouraged them to follow him into his office. "To be fair, I wasn't completely sure you would make it this far. It's been my experience that when people are confronted with a subject that makes them feel even the slightest bit uncomfortable, they tend to scurry as fast as possible towards what they perceive to be a more pleasant direction. Anyway, I'm very happy you've decided to stick around. You might not want to hear this but I've been giving this a lot of thought and here's what I think we are up against... I believe that the plaintiffs actually have a legitimate case."

"What do you mean?" Adam panicked.

"I'm not trying to scare you but I would rather be honest and upfront with you from the very beginning."

"We certainly appreciate your candor, Mr. Randall," Clare said succinctly.

"The basis of their argument will be that because you refused to bake them a wedding cake, they feel that you violated their civil liberties."

"We were simply acting according to our beliefs," Clare reminded him.

"I totally understand that, however, there are a few things that might be problematic. At the top of the list; your bakery is open to the public and one of the services that you provide, is making wedding cakes."

"Okay..." Clare interrupted.

"Second", Josh said ignoring her, "the plaintiff came into your shop to enlist your help".

Both Clare and Adam nodded in agreement.

"Third, you were more than willing to accommodate him all the way up until the point you found out that this was for a gay wedding at which time you refused to help. Is this an accurate assessment?"

"Yes, but..."

Josh stopped Clare yet again, before she could finish.

"Look, it is my job to anticipate what direction this will take in court. The attorney for the plaintiffs will do his best to paint a picture of you as not only homophobes, but bigots as well."

"We are most certainly not bigots, Mr. Randall." Clare proclaimed in a defiant tone.

"I didn't say that you were," Josh said in a soothing and reassuring voice. "They are trying to win this case. If they are successful in convincing even one or two jurors that the real reason behind your actions was malice, then they will succeed in their mission."

"But that's not true," Adam protested.

"Doesn't matter," said Josh. "In the confines of a courtroom, everything is primarily a matter of perception."

"Oh" Clare thoughtfully murmured, trying her best to digest what Josh had just said.

"Please do not misunderstand me," Josh pleaded, "I'm not trying to be argumentative here but once this goes to court, the plaintiffs will definitely want to get you on the witness stand."

"We would welcome the opportunity to defend our beliefs," Adam asserted.

"I don't think you realize what you are getting yourselves into. Have either of you ever been in a courtroom before?"

"No" they both uttered, almost in unison.

"Well, it is the job of the plaintiff's attorney to discredit you on the witness stand and he will do whatever he can to make you look as though you are in the wrong."

"I suspected as much," said Adam. "But we are not afraid. We feel that God wants us to tell our side of the story."

"And what story might that be?" Josh asked, trying not to sound too disparaging.

"That marriage is supposed to be between a man and a woman." Clare said defiantly.

"You do realize that once you are on the stand, I will not be able to control what happens."

"We are not ashamed of the Lord, Mr. Randall." Clare reminded him.

"I never said, nor did I mean to imply that you were. A skillful attorney, however, will do his very best to shake you."

"Nothing can deter our faith," said Adam.

"I have to warn you," Josh cautioned, "this isn't going to be easy. You might find this entire experience painful. Once this trial gets underway you need to be prepared that your fundamental beliefs are going to be challenged every step of the way and as I had mentioned before, the attorney for the plaintiffs will try his best to make you appear to be bigoted."

"We are not bigots. We believe that God loves everyone equally regardless of race, gender or skin color," Clare stressed.

"You forgot to mention sexual orientation." Josh added for good measure.

"For this is the will of God, your sanctification: that you abstain from sexual immorality," Clare said with authority, and then added "first Thessalonians four three."

Josh patiently waited for Clare to finish her mini sermon. "I realize that you may have a thorough grasp of the bible, and you are not afraid to toss out verses as need be, but once we are in that courtroom, I'm going to have to ask you to refrain from bringing up the bible or quoting passages."

Clare tried to suppress her frustration. "The bible contains nothing but truth, how can this be a problem?"

"Don't you see, to non-believers using the bible is at best, a circular definition. You can't say something is true because it is written in the bible and when questioned about it: you try to validate your claim by pointing to another passage that states that everything contained in the bible is true."

Clare looked at him as though he was deliberately trying to annoy her.

"Best case scenario," Josh theorized, "is that there might be three, maybe four people on that jury who are Christians. If the majority of the people on that jury don't subscribe to your beliefs, then to the rest of the jury, you might as well be quoting from a copy of Mother Goose's Nursery Rhymes."

Clare could feel her blood starting to boil. "How could you possibly equate Mother Goose to the Word of God?"

"You can't introduce anything in court without establishing its validity. There is no way we are going to have the time to prove the validity of the bible."

Doing his best to defuse the situation, Josh decided to switch subjects.

"How long have you owned your bakery?"

"Going on nine years now" Adam said with pride.

"So you guys are pretty adept at making pastries?"

"We'd like to think so," Clare bragged, as she let her anger drift away.

"I'm sure you guys are quite good at what you do," Josh reassured them. "Although it may not seem like it now; my particular skill set, if you could call it that; lies in the fact that I am pretty good at getting people to go down the path I would like them to take. I believe if you ask the right questions; more often than not, you can get the right answers."

"And what are the right answers Mr. Randall?" Clare asked, as if she were a principal schooling an unruly child.

"I never said that I have all the answers," Josh asserted, while refusing to take the bait. "And if you are expecting me to provide some sort of feel-good secret insight as to how the universe works, you're definitely barking up the wrong tree."

Before Clare could respond, Josh challenged. "Am I correct in assuming that you would like to win this case?"

"Of course."

"Okay, let me break it down for you. The attorney for the defendants will argue that by refusing to bake a wedding cake for his clients, you violated their civil rights. This is a fact that we can't argue."

"I thought you were on our side?" Adam complained.

"I am. But you did refuse to bake them a cake."

"Yes, but we didn't refuse to serve Mr. Addicott as a customer, we simply said we did not feel comfortable making him a wedding cake." Clare argued in her defense.

"Why is that?"

"Because we happen to believe in God's word, Mr. Randall," Adam emphasized.

"I'm sorry," Josh said, while tapping his chest, "I've actually read the bible more than once, and I don't ever recall reading a verse that said...Thou Shalt Not Bake Wedding Cakes For Gays."

"Do not make a mockery of the Lord, Mr. Randall," Clare cautioned, as she wagged her index finger. "We simply do not wish to condone sinful behavior."

"Fair enough," Josh acknowledged, as he held up his hand. "I'm not the enemy here. But once you are on that stand, I may be able to object to a certain line of questioning but ultimately you are going to be the ones defending your actions."

"We are not ashamed of our actions, Mr. Randall. We believe that God's laws take precedence over man made laws," Adam declared.

Josh thought about it for a moment. "If you are adamant about presenting your views, then maybe we should get the plaintiff to admit that his beliefs are important."

"How could that possibly help?" Adam asked with all the curiosity of an eager, honor roll student.

"Everybody on this planet has some sort of beliefs, even if you don't subscribe to the idea that there is a God, we all have opinions about how the world works and why we are here. We are arguing that your beliefs stem from a Higher Power – am I correct in this?"

"Of course," Clare affirmed.

"I can't say for certain, but once they acknowledge that their beliefs are equally as important: and their actions are guided by what they perceive to be the truth, I imagine we should be able to circle back around to why the first amendment is so important to this country. It may sound like I'm going out on a limb here, but I am asking you to trust that I know what I am doing."

"No one is trying to insinuate that you are not a competent attorney," Adam said, trying his best to appease him.

Josh ignored Adam's blatant attempt to suck up to him and instead, politely smiled. "We still have lots of ground to cover and I tend to think better on a full stomach. Is it okay with you if we finish this conversation while we eat lunch?"

Clare and Adam looked at each other as if they had been offered an invitation to witness a satanic ritual.

Josh held up his hand. "It's only lunch, a nice family restaurant …okay?"

Clare looked at Adam for some sort of sign and sensing that it would be acceptable she reluctantly said "I suppose so."

a house divided

"You seem a bit relieved that I didn't bring you to the same restaurant as the last time."

Clare sighed pleasantly, as Josh held the door for them to enter the Applebee's. The hostess brought them to a booth in the back corner of the restaurant.

As they were walking to their table, "it is nothing personal Mr. Randall, it's just that we happen to view the world differently that's all." Clare honestly stated.

"And how might you view the world?" Josh asked in earnest.

"What I think Clare meant to say, is that we try to see things through God's eyes."

"Do your best to present yourself to God as one approved, a worker who has no need to be ashamed, rightly handling the word of truth." Clare said, with authority.

"I don't mean to keep on harping on you," Josh pointed out, "but why do you feel the necessity to quote from the bible?"

"Do you have a problem with God's Word?" Adam speculated.

"Not at all, but for some silly reason I get the feeling that you think that if you regurgitate scriptures it will automatically help others understand the truth. You might as well have a bumper sticker on your car saying that Jesus Saves. Think about it," Josh continued. "Who is going to see that sticker and understand the message? Jesus saves what? Jesus saves money? Jesus saves newspapers? Jesus saves coupons?"

"I don't know what type of game you are trying to play Mr. Randall," Clare said emphatically, "but I don't appreciate it one bit."

"Although I do enjoy having fun," Josh freely acknowledged, "I can assure you that this is not a game, the stakes are far too high. I take my work very seriously. I believe that if you can successfully lead the jurors far enough down the right path: hopefully they will have no other choice but to come to the only logical conclusion."

"You can lead a horse to water..."

Josh interrupted Adam before he could finish his train of thought. "That's an excellent point, and I love the fact that you brought up such a great analogy because drinking water is essential for life. I happen to think that if you can get someone close enough to see the water, dip their fingers and toes into it, at some point I believe that they might be curious enough to taste the water and once they try it, they will understand that this water quenches their thirst. Look, I'm sure you've heard of the expression preaching to the choir, right?"

"Of course," Clare affirmed.

"Well, for me it means preaching to those who are already in agreement. If you are really trying to reach people who don't believe, quoting scriptures from a book that means nothing to them probably won't help."

"And what would you suggest Mr. Randall?" Clare interjected, as if trying to understand how Josh could be so mixed up.

"I'm not trying to fight you on this. I know you may have your suspicions about me, but the truth is we are on the same page. I simply believe that you may be going about it in the wrong way. Sadly, I think that some Christians act as though they are morally superior to everyone else. Being an atheist or agnostic does not automatically make one morally bankrupt. In fact, I am certain that there are some wonderful, decent, honest human beings who just don't happen to believe in God. If your goal is to reach the unreached, you can't be afraid to go where they are. And for the record, acting as though your shit doesn't stink won't help either."

Clare wrinkled her nose and recoiled at the image.

"Look, you seem like really nice people and I am sure you have the best of intentions, but don't you think you are wasting far too much energy trying give off the illusion that you've achieved perfection? Sadly, we live in a world in which sometimes people will swear. This is a fact of life: you need to get over it. I realize I am pointing out the obvious here but I am a work in progress. Once in a while, okay most of the time, my actions will fall far short of perfection. I understand that my occasional use of profanity may upset your delicate sensibilities, so for your sake, I will try my best to tone it down a bit. However, just to be on the safe side, I am going to apologize ahead of time in case I slip up and my language gets too colorful."

Josh decided his best course of action would be to try to smooth things over. "Let me ask you... when did you become Christians?"

Finally, a safe topic, Clare thought. She happily volunteered, "For me, it was my senior year in high school."

"And I was a sophomore in college. We actually met in bible study." Adam looked at Clare lovingly, as he fondly remembered when they first met.

"I'm so very happy for you," Josh proclaimed, but it didn't sound as convincing as he had hoped. "And since that time have you been perfect?"

"We try to live Godly lives." Adam said, with all sincerity.

"That's not what I asked you."

"Nobody's perfect, Mr. Randall." Clare said in defense.

"Exactly," Josh asserted. "We are all flawed human beings and since we are all unique individuals, doesn't it make sense that we all have our own set of trials and tribulations that we need to go through?"

"But the bible says..."

Josh put up his hand, cutting Clare off midstream. "Since becoming Christians, have you led a perfect life?" He repeated.

"No, of course not," Adam readily conceded.

"So, you are admitting that in spite of everything you know, you still sin?" Josh hinted.

"At no time have I ever tried to claim that I never sin," Clare said defiantly. "But when I do sin, I am repentant."

"Seriously, that's your game plan? When you find yourself standing before God, are you really planning on telling Him that because you have repented of your sins, you believe that He has entrusted you with the task of judging others?"

"We are not judging Mr. Randall, we are merely pointing out what it says…"

Once again, Josh interrupted her before she could complete her sentence. "I know, I know … you were repeating what it says in the bible," he said, in an almost condescending tone.

"Yes," Clare confirmed.

"So that's how you justify your thought process? That's kind of like going up to a rather hefty woman and saying I don't mean to offend you but if you decided to eat less, you probably wouldn't be so fat."

"It's not the same thing and you know it," Clare fumed.

"Okay, it might not be exactly the same, but if you start off the conversation by pointing out what you perceive to be their flaws, you probably won't get too far. You can't have it both ways. Maybe I'm being naïve about this, but I really don't think anyone is less worthy of God's love simply because they have a different set of struggles than I do."

Adam exhaled loudly. "Who said anything about being less worthy?" As he was desperately trying to figure out where this conversation was going.

"I may not have biblical verses memorized like you do: but in all the passages I have read about Jesus, I cannot recall Him ever saying if you first repent, then and only then - will I think about healing you."

Both Clare and Adam looked equally bewildered at Josh's biblical interpretation.

"I believe that people really do want to know the truth but they don't want to be preached at. No one wants to be told that they are wrong about their beliefs. It's just human nature. If you want to guarantee that someone will stop listening, start the conversation off by telling them everything they believe in, is wrong. You could be giving them all the wisdom of the world, and more than likely, it will never sink in."

Adam and Clare were dumbfounded. Josh was supposed to be their attorney they thought to themselves. How could he be badgering them like this?

"If you are really trying to convert someone to your way of thinking you will never win an argument by insulting them first."

"I never insulted anyone," Clare said emphatically.

"Never?" Josh let it slide. "Maybe insulted is the wrong word but if you start off by insisting that you are right, it forces people into a corner where they will feel obligated to defend their beliefs."

"I think I understand what you are doing," Adam concluded. "The trick is how do you get someone to think about God without forcing it down their throat?"

"That's about the size of it," Josh affirmed, feeling a bit vindicated.

Clare was still fuming. "Since you seem to think you have all the answers," she said smugly. "How would you go about it?"

"Why not try a little kindness? Why not simply try being their friend? Sometimes people need to know how much you care, before they care about how much you know. If you really want to help someone understand the truth, you have to be willing to exercise a little patience. It seems to me, like you're extremely proud and itching to announce that you are a Christian."

"Why wouldn't we be?" Clare asked as she was becoming more irritated with each insinuation.

"Maybe I phrased that wrong, I am not saying that you shouldn't be except..." Josh paused to think of the exact words. "I would have to say for me, I feel blessed. To say that the odds were stacked against me would be an understatement. I was one of those people who had no use for God. It wasn't that I hated the idea of a Supreme Being; I figured that if God helped you get through your day, then good for you. I guess, looking back on it, I suppose my beliefs were something akin to ... If there really was a God; then it goes without saying that He would know that deep down inside I wasn't an evil person."

Clare and Adam just looked at one another wondering how he could be so mixed up.

"Look around you," Josh urged them. "What percentage of people in this restaurant do you think are Christians?"

"I would say maybe thirty percent," Adam volunteered.

"I think you're being generous," said Josh. "But let's say for arguments sake, you are right. Here's the problem I see ... seventy percent of not only the patrons in this restaurant, but seventy percent of the entire world think that you are wrong."

Josh paused to give them time to reflect upon what he had just said.

"What are there, four maybe five major religions in the world? You have the Hindus over here," Josh picked up a ketchup bottle and moved it over to the right-hand corner of the table. Next Josh picked up the mustard container. "Here we have the Buddhists," and he moved the squeeze bottle over to the opposite side of the table. Josh proceeded to pick up a napkin. "Let's say that this napkin represents Judaism." He gently placed the napkin in front of Clare. Josh then picked up the pepper shaker. "Let's say that this shaker represents Islam," and moved the pepper in front of Adam. "Here we have Christianity," Josh picked up the salt shaker and placed it in the center of the table.

"Oops, I almost forgot." Josh picked up a little square box containing multiple packets of sugar and artificial sweeteners. "And over here we have the Scientologists, Pagans and New Age believers. Now to complicate matters," Josh picked up the salt shaker and sprinkled a little on the table. "Christianity can be further broken down into several different denominations."

Josh picked up his fork and started pointing the prongs at each one of the little individual grains. "Here you have Baptists, Catholics, Lutherans, Protestants, Methodists, Episcopalians ... each and every one all claiming to have a monopoly on the truth."

Both Clare and Adam looked at one another, equally confused with where this demonstration was going.

"Could you really imagine a Quaker saying ... We Quakers have a pretty good grasp on the truth. We probably have it about ninety-five or ninety-six percent correct, but those Amish across the street, they are one hundred percent right on the money?"

"Not really," Adam said thoughtfully.

"Of course not, it wouldn't make any sense. If the Quakers knew the Amish were one hundred percent correct, wouldn't the Quakers want to be Amish as well?"

"I guess," Adam confirmed after a brief moment of introspection.

"Now, I want you to envision of all the patrons in this restaurant as being either atheists or agnostics. They look over at this table and they think we are all idiots, because they understand that every single one of us is fully convinced that we KNOW the truth." Josh held up a ketchup bottle. "Wouldn't you expect that all Hindus believe that they are on the right path?"

"I suppose so," Clare reluctantly agreed.

"And what about..." as Josh picks up the mustard container, "the Buddhists?"

"I see your point," said Adam.

"It is no wonder that most atheists think that we're all ridiculous. You have to concede that at least they are smart enough to understand the law of non-contradiction. They have enough common sense to realize that unless we all believe the exact same thing; it is impossible for everyone to be right. How could any sane, rational human being think that you could have completely opposing views and still end up in the very same place?"

After Josh put all the items back in their proper places, there remained a few sprinkles of salt in the center of the table.

"Maybe Jesus was trying to tell His followers that if we waste all of our time and energy insisting that it is only OUR own particular faction that really matters, instead of concentrating on the truth, then we will end up rendering ourselves useless." With that he brushed the salt unto the floor.

When the waitress came over, Josh looked at her name tag and said, "Bailey, what a pretty name. Bailey, I have to apologize; I spilt a little salt and I'm sorry for messing up your floor."

She looked at him as though he had rocks in his head. Why would anyone apologize for such a trivial matter she thought to herself?

After she had finished taking everyone's order, Josh said "I was wondering if you would do me a huge favor. I haven't done my good deed for the day. See that table over there..."

"Which one?"

"The one right over there," as Josh discretely pointed with his pinky to the table with four gentlemen all wearing military uniforms.

"Yeah" she nodded.

Josh handed Bailey a twenty, "This is for you. When they are ready to pay, could you do me a favor and bring their bill over to me before you give it to them..."

"Okay...I guess," was all she could muster.

"Thank you so very much."

No sooner had Bailey left the table, Josh resumed the conversation without missing a beat.

"I think that most people try to be good, they teach their kids not to lie and not to steal but they never really take the time to think about why."

Adam and Clare looked at one another thoughtfully.

"However, now's not the time to get into a theological discussion," Josh said. "We've got way too much work to do and if we are going to win this case, we need to focus on the task at hand. You remember I told you that the attorney for the plaintiffs will do his best to discredit you?"

"Yes," Clare acknowledged, as Adam was nodding his head.

"Well, if I was in his shoes, I would assume that there would be at least a couple of atheists on the jury. I would start off by doing my best to discredit or nullify the first amendment."

"What do you mean discredit the first amendment?" Adam inquired, hoping to gain some sort of insight.

Josh thought about it for a moment, "I imagine that most people tend to think of their religion as the source of truth. That being said, it is possible that the first amendment could be interpreted in such a manner that all beliefs must be regarded as equal. Are you willing to concede that all of the major religions have different convictions?"

"I'm certain of it," Clare revealed.

"Good," Josh agreed. "Well, what if your religion told you not to associate with Jews?

"It doesn't," said Adam.

"But you understand that there might be other religions that might subscribe to this doctrine?"

"Then they would be wrong," Clare demanded.

"I just want you to imagine, if you hung a sign on the door that said NO JEWS ALLOWED, could you see where this would be a good argument against the first amendment?"

"How so?" Clare said thoughtfully.

"Well imagine if your god told you to do something that violated another person's rights?"

"Yes, but we didn't do that," Adam insisted.

Josh stared at him in disbelief. It is truly amazing; he thought to himself how oblivious some people can be. "If I were the attorney for the plaintiffs, I would argue that everyone's beliefs are equal. A Buddhist has exactly the same right to his or her beliefs as a Muslim or a Christian or even a Jew. Under the first amendment, we are all guaranteed the right to freely exercise our religion." Josh held his finger up and paused..."Even atheists."

"But doesn't that help to prove our case?" Clare speculated.

"It does, except for one tiny little problem. Everyone's views are different. We all see the world in a slightly different way. Even if you have two Christians in the same room, it is virtually impossible to get them to agree on absolutely everything."

"Why is that so important?" Adam inquired, feeling even more confused.

"Because we live in a society where we are all guaranteed certain rights. My rights are equally as important as your rights," said Josh. "Are you following me so far?"

"I think we are keeping up," Clare insisted.

"The plaintiffs are going to try to argue that even though you are claiming religious freedom; your rights should not supersede their rights."

"I think I understand where you are going with this," Adam said astutely. "But I thought you said we had a good case?"

"We actually do, but we have to go back to the U.S. Constitution. Our founding fathers understood how important one's beliefs really are. They intuitively knew that it would be morally wrong for the government to compel any of its citizens to disregard their own personal values. Imagine a pregnant woman being allowed to sue a Christian doctor because he refused to perform an abortion. Just because someone runs a business, doesn't mean that they should be forced to violate their beliefs. I believe what the attorney for the plaintiffs may try to do is persuade the jury that there are major flaws in almost all religions, therefore there is a fundamental flaw in the first amendment."

From the blank stares given by both Adam and Clare, Josh knew he had confused them even more.

"The first amendment guarantees everyone the freedom to worship your God the way you see fit. The problem I see is, what happens when my beliefs differ from yours? Should my beliefs be able to negate or supersede your beliefs?"

Josh continued, "Suppose my religion tells me that we all were given freewill. That everyone on this planet has the freedom to accept or reject God, it is completely up to us. Now imagine if there was another religion that states if you refuse to follow the exact tenants prescribed in its holy book, you should be put to death."

"But Christianity doesn't subscribe to that belief," said Clare.

"But maybe some religions do," Josh challenged.

"Then," Adam declared, "they would be wrong,"

"I'm not disputing that, but can't you see how someone could argue that the first amendment guarantees you the right to worship as you see fit and if your religion tells you it is permissible to kill non-believers, then your beliefs would actually infringe on the rights of others?"

"That kind of makes sense," Adam acknowledged. "But we are not forcing anyone to put their trust in God, and we certainly are not advocating killing those who refuse to accept our faith."

"Let's just say that when it comes to the first amendment, the law considers everyone's beliefs to be equally important. If I were the attorney for the plaintiffs, and I was not able to successfully point out the flaws with some religions, another avenue I might take, would be to discredit you and make you look like hypocrites to the jury."

"But we are not hypocrites," Adam vehemently protested.

"I'm not saying that you are, but once again, as soon as you are on that witness stand their attorney will do his best to attack your character."

"We are not ashamed of either our actions or our beliefs," Clare reminded Josh in a defiant tone.

"Again, I'm not trying to insinuate that you should be. Look, I'm fairly certain that you are aware that over the centuries, the bible has been interpreted differently."

"So..."

"Well, let's just say that perhaps not all people view things in exactly the same way."

"What are you trying to imply Mr. Randall?" Adam challenged.

"You needn't to get so defensive. I'm simply trying to understand where you are coming from. You believe that by refusing to bake a cake for a gay wedding you are doing God's will...yes?"

"That's correct." Clare agreed.

"Don't you think that on September 11, 2001, those nineteen hijackers who flew the planes into the twin towers also believed they were doing God's will." Josh speculated, hoping to elicit an emotion.

Clare fell for the ploy hook, line and sinker. "We didn't kill thousands of innocent people. How could you possibly equate the two?"

"Although both you and I may understand this; but to those who are uncertain about their beliefs, it is quite possible that they think we are all praying to the exact same God, we are just calling Him different names such as Buddha or Allah."

"How could anyone think that a loving God would ever want you to kill innocent people?" Adam asked, looking quite bewildered.

"I am not an expert on the Quran," said Josh, "but obviously there is something in the text that made the jihadists feel compelled to take the actions that they did."

Up until this very moment, Clare had never given much thought about the religion of Islam. "If God is capable of creating the entire universe," she speculated, "that means He created EVERYTHING ... Why on earth would anyone believe that God would create something He hated? It doesn't make any sense. Why don't people understand that a loving and perfect God would never leave behind a book that inspired His followers to hate and kill others?"

"I think that when it comes to all religions, some people tend to fixate on passages they like and ignore the ones they do not." Josh said thoughtfully.

Before Josh could finish the conversation, Bailey arrived with their orders.

Sensing that Josh might try to forgo the customary prayer before eating, Clare reached out for his hand

and quickly blurted out a quick prayer. "Thank you, dear Lord, for the nourishment you are about to provide. Thank you for all the blessings you've bestowed upon us. Help us to walk in a manner worthy of these gifts. We pray this in your precious name, Amen."

Clare looked up at Josh's stunned facial expression and said, "You disapprove of the way we worship Mr. Randall?"

"Disapprove is not the word I would have chosen." Josh replied, truthfully.

"Please, don't hold back," Clare snapped.

"I'm just wondering who benefits from this public display?" Josh said pragmatically. "I am not trying to imply that it is somehow wrong to be thankful for all the blessings you have: but it almost feels like you believe that if you make a show of praying before you eat, perhaps everyone watching will immediately understand that you must know the truth about God"

"It doesn't matter what they think." Adam proclaimed bluntly.

"I'd have to say yes and no." Josh said, trying his best not to confuse them. "By that I mean – if they looked over and thought we were all idiots, in the grand scheme of things it wouldn't make much of a difference. If, however, this was their very last meal on this planet, for us not to care about them seems to me, to be a bit cold and callous."

Josh continued his theological discussion. "The other night when we first met, you seemed a bit offended because I ordered a beer."

"And do not get drunk with wine, for that is debauchery, but be filled with the spirit." Clare reminded him.

"I don't think God ever once said Thou Shalt Never Drink Alcohol. I understand that moderation is important. If all we do is drink to excess, we end up wasting our lives and we have nothing left to do but imagine what could have been." Josh continued, "I could be completely wrong about this, but I highly doubt that you could entice throngs of people to understand that they really should take the time to learn God's Word if you start the conversation off by pointing out how you disapprove of their lifestyle. To me, it sounds an awful lot like judging."

Adam squeezed Clare's hand beneath the table.

Josh could not hold his tongue any longer. "Do you really think that by going around and quoting scriptures, it will make you a better Christian? Did you ever stop to think that to the outside world, it might make you look arrogant and self-righteous?"

"We are not concerned with how the outside world looks at us." Adam affirmed, coming to his wife's defense.

Josh could practically feel Clare's eyes burning into his soul.

"You may not approve of my drinking, you may not like the fact that I choose to use colorful language, but isn't that something that God should be judging me on?"

"Oh, He will." Clare reminded him.

"I'm sorry that I'm not perfect. I realize that I may not be as well-spoken as you would like. You think that because you refuse to swear, that somehow nonbelievers will instinctively understand that you know everything there is to know about the truth? The world is a messy place, people drink, people swear and people enjoy sex. I'm quite certain that I may have vocalized this before, but people don't want to feel judged, they want to feel loved. I think that's just human nature. If we, as Christians, are unwilling to love someone unconditionally, they will automatically gravitate towards those who do."

Clare could feel the blood rushing to the capillaries in her face as Josh continued to lay into them.

"Let me ask you, do you remember the first miracle performed by Jesus in the Gospel of John? Just in case your memory is a bit hazy, the first miracle He performed was to turn water into wine. He could have chosen to turn it into lemonade or any other sort of liquidy beverage, yet He chose to turn it into wine. Now perhaps everybody at the wedding was using the wine for bathing but I really don't think so. You will never get anyone to even want to learn about the truth, if you first insist on pointing out what behaviors you dislike."

"These are God's commands," Clare asserted. "Not mine."

"Okay, but if someone doesn't believe in God, why should they feel the need to modify their behavior?"

"Are you finished?" Clare demanded as politely as she could, under the circumstances.

"Not quite, there are millions, if not billions of hard-working people who are trying their best to live their lives in a respectable and decent manner yet for one reason or another, they don't see the world as you do."

"That doesn't make them right," Adam informed him.

"I completely agree, but try to look at it objectively. Instead of trying to demand that they change their behavior to conform to what you think is proper; why not start by simply loving them? Why would you want to skip the most important step? You really don't need to worry about anything else. It isn't very complicated; the fact of the matter is that people want to be loved for who they are."

"But God hates sin." Clare protested.

"I'm not trying to insinuate that He doesn't; just try to consider it in terms of a mathematical equation. You can't expect people to understand advanced calculus or trigonometry without first helping them understand the basic numerical fundamentals such as addition and subtraction. When you really boil Christianity down to its purest form, it all starts with love. I believe that once people realize that they are loved unconditionally, they will be more susceptible to understanding the truth. Perhaps then, they will freely choose to modify their behavior."

From the glazed look in their eyes, Josh felt the conversation starting to slip further away and paused to let them catch up.

"Again, I am not trying to argue that you are wrong about your beliefs, I'm just saying that if you go around acting holier than thou and quoting scriptures, the only people who will really hear you are those who are already in agreement."

Feeling the need to defend his wife, "Do not have fellowship with sin, but reprove it. Ephesians: five eleven." Adam added thoughtfully.

"How very nice," Josh said sarcastically. "You have a list of biblical verses at your disposal to throw out at anyone whenever it suits your purpose. It is no wonder that Christianity is on the decline. Have you ever heard the expression about not being able to see the forest from the trees? You walk around quoting passages and you know what most outsiders see?"

"And what do you think they see?" Clare demanded, while trying to suppress her rising anger.

"Instead of seeing you as this wonderful, pious person who should be emulated; maybe they see someone who is pretentious and conceited."

"We don't have to take this Mr. Randall." Adam jumped in.

"You're absolutely right, you don't," Josh divulged. "But I told you, once you are on the witness stand the attorney for the plaintiffs is going to do his very best to get under your skin. This is just the tip of the iceberg."

The conversation was wearing Clare down, her mind was reeling. She wasn't certain if this was Josh expressing his own thoughts about them, or if he was just playing devil's advocate.

"I'm sorry that I am deliberately being confrontational." Josh said, "but you've got to expect this when you are on the witness stand. And just for the record, I was playing nice."

"You call that nice?" Clare protested, trying to regain her composure.

As if on cue, Bailey arrived with the lunch tab from the table full of servicemen. "Here's the receipt you requested," and she handed it to Josh.

Josh pulled out a pen from his jacket pocket and quickly scribbled, "Thank You For Your Service! God Loves You" and he handed it back to Bailey along with a hundred-dollar bill. "This should cover it."

"I'll be right back with your change."

"Nope, the rest is yours."

Bailey looked down at the bill, did some quick mental arithmetic and gave Josh a beaming smile.

"Thank you," she mumbled silently.

"The pleasure was all mine," Josh said in a soothing tone.

When Bailey handed the paid receipt to the gentlemen, she pointed back towards Josh.

Everyone at the table gratefully smiled and waved thanks.

Josh smiled back, nodded his head in recognition and held up his hand as if to say it was all good.

As she watched the scene unfold, Clare could feel her blood pressure coming back to normal.

"That was a very nice gesture, Mr. Randall." Clare confessed, and then added, "I'm a bit curious though, why didn't you write ... Jesus loves you?"

"Don't you think you are putting the cart before the horse?"

"What do you mean?" she asked.

"Think about it," Josh explained, "if you are talking to someone who doesn't believe in God, don't you think that trying to get them to accept that Jesus is His Son might be skipping a few steps? Imagine it this way; you have to think of yourself as a farmer. If you eventually want to harvest your crop, it probably would be a good idea to start off by planting a few seeds."

For some inexplicable reason, the metaphor was completely lost on Clare.

"I really don't want to get side tracked here, let's try to stay focused on the upcoming trial. I don't believe in sugar coating things, as I was saying earlier, the odds are that there will probably be as many as three or four atheists on the jury. We have to anticipate that some of them may think of you as gullible or foolish at best. As a species, we human beings tend to be very selfish. We tend to put our wants and needs before those of others. We also tend to value our own opinions. Most people, myself included, do not like to think that they are wrong."

"We are not wrong about this," Adam emphasized. "This is God's Word."

"That's exactly what I am talking about," Josh asserted. "The problem I see with making a statement like that, is to an outsider, it might make you appear to be extremely arrogant. Wouldn't all Muslims want to make the exact same claim? Don't you think that all Hindus or Buddhists believe they are on the right path? Insisting that you are right, does very little to help anyone understand. You don't get it, no one wants to have any sort of theology shoved down their throat."

"Who said anything about shoving it down their throat?"

"To a non-believer that's what it kind of feels like. It feels as though you are screaming that their beliefs are wrong and your views are right. Most people don't like to consider themselves to be stupid, so more often than not, when someone starts talking about religion, we might think to ourselves ... what makes you so smart? If you are not living an absolutely perfect life, what sticks out like a neon sign, is your hypocrisy."

"Imagine a dirty, drunken homeless man with just three teeth," Josh continued. "Two on the bottom and one on the top...who reeks of urine and body odor. Imagine if he were to stumble up to a stranger and start slurring about how much Jesus loves you. Do you really think the average person would want to stick around and here what he has to say?"

Clare's head was swimming. Every time she thought she knew where the conversation was going, Josh took it in another direction.

"If you were born a Muslim or Hindu or Buddhist, this would probably be the only religion you would have ever known. Why would you ever think to question the authenticity behind it? Why would anyone ever think their parents would set out to deliberately lie to or mislead them?"

"No one said that they would intentionally lie," Clare said defensively.

"Let's say for the time being," Adam offered up as a possible solution, "we simply accept they are misguided."

"I like that term," Josh said, and he repeated the word. "Misguided." Josh thought about it for a moment. "Let me put it this way, I think that you would be foolish not to admire people of other faiths. In fact, many devout Muslims have such a deep-seated desire to live their lives for their god, that it puts the faith of many Christians to shame."

Before Adam could get another word in edgewise, Josh continued. "But once someone has a hunger to know the truth, I believe that they should be willing to examine their faith from every angle. If it is indeed the truth, it wouldn't make any sense if it contained anything that contradicted a pure and Holy God."

"Don't you think that they would realize," Clare added, as she thought about some of the different beliefs other religions subscribe to, "that a loving God would never call on his followers to kill others?"

"Common sense tells me so, but I suspect that the majority of people never really take the time to scrutinize their beliefs. It is almost as if people are content to go through life with giant blinders on. While they may suspect that something isn't quite right or that there is something missing; for some unknown reason, they are unwilling to search for the truth."

"I still don't see what all this has to do with our case," said Clare.

"When this case goes to trial, once you are on that witness stand, the attorney for the plaintiffs will be attacking your beliefs non-stop. I want you to be prepared, that your interpretation of God's Word will be questioned."

"We are more than ready to defend our beliefs," Adam said with conviction.

"Please don't make the assumption," Josh added, "that the plaintiff's attorney will not have a working knowledge of the bible. Remember, he argues for a living. He will do his homework."

"We are quite confident that we are interpreting our beliefs correctly," Clare assured him.

Josh looked at Clare and resisted the urge to question her. "Like it or not, your refusal to bake that wedding cake did technically violate their right to be treated equally."

"I thought we had moved on from this point," said Adam.

"Sorry, bad habit of mine. Sometimes I think aloud. I do believe that we have the law on our side but we definitely have some work to do." Josh looked down at his watch, "I'd love to converse some more about this, but I've got to get back to the office. I'm going to email you a list of possible questions I think their attorney will be asking you at the trial, so at the very least, you won't be caught off guard when you are on the witness stand. Do you have any more questions for me right now?"

Both Adam and Clare shook their heads no.

"Then I've got this taken care of on my end, if you think of anything, please do not hesitate to send me a text or shoot me an email. Other than that, I will see you on the 17th."

"Thank you once again for taking on this case," Adam said sincerely. "We truly do appreciate your help."

"No need to thank me, I haven't done anything yet."

"Just the same," Clare politely acknowledged, "thank you."

"Don't mention it." Josh said, as he deposited three twenties and a ten on the bill and left them sitting at the table.

all things must pass

Instead of heading back to the office, Josh pointed his Acura towards home. "Siri call Susan."

The phone rang and a voice said "Hi Honey"

"Hey, it's me," as if she wouldn't know. "Thinking about calling it an early day, do we need anything before I come home?"

"Nothing comes to mind. Is everything all right?"

"Everything's fine, just a bit taxing. I dropped Paco off this morning and just finished up with the Robinsons."

"And?"

"I'm not really sure if they know what they are getting themselves into that's all."

"I'm sure everything will work out fine," Susan said, cheerfully.

"I'm glad one of us has confidence."

"Me too" she said smiling into the phone.

"I'll fill you in on all the gory details when I get home. Love you."

"Love you more," Susan said honestly.

Josh hung up the phone and cranked up the volume on the stereo. He immediately recognized the unmistakable opening notes from Jerry's steel guitar leading up to the polished harmonizing of Crosby, Stills, Nash and Young. What a perfect song Josh thought to himself.

put your house in order

The following Friday, Josh pulled into the visitors parking spot just outside the front entrance. Looking around at the beautiful facilities he thought to himself, not a bad place to dry out. He gave Paco a huge bear hug as soon as he came walking around the corner.

"Wow. You clean up nice, I have to say you look pretty darned good for somebody in the midst of detoxing. How are you holding up?"

"The people are nice enough but I gotta tell ya," Paco said in a somewhat hushed voice, "this place is depressing."

"What do you mean?"

They walked over to the leather couch and sat down away from any possible snooping ears.

"Some of the crap that these people have been through: it actually makes you want to do drugs just to forget about it."

"I can only imagine."

"I thought I had seen a lot but..." Paco's voice trailed off. "There's this one girl, she's a cutter. You know, slices up her arms. I guess the physical pain helps her to forget her emotional pain. Anyway, her stepdad started molesting her when she was just five."

"Wow that sucks." Josh said, shaking his head in sadness. "Is he in jail now?"

"I don't think so. I'm pretty sure they're divorced but it is still a sucky way to grow up."

"Tell me about it."

"Poor kid's all messed up. She blames her mother because she didn't protect her."

"That's a pretty normal response."

"No shit."

"The world's a messy place my friend." Josh said as if offering up the secret of the universe.

"Nah, some people just suck." Paco said, with all the authority of one who truly knows.

"Can't argue with that one," Josh readily agreed. "So how are you holding up?"

"Not too bad. There is a shitload of therapy sessions. Most of the day is spent listening to other people's sob stories."

"Are you learning anything?"

"I'm learning I don't want to come back."

"At least it's a start Paco; at least it's a start. Before I forget, did you talk to your dad?"

"Yeah."

"How'd that go?"

"He wasn't happy if that's what you are asking."

"Did you really think he was going to be?"

"I suppose not."

"And?"

"He got over it."

"Somehow I knew he would." Instead of ignoring the elephant in the room, Josh decided to tackle the subject virtually head on. "You know that shit is bad news."

"What?" Paco pretended not to understand what his friend was saying. "Yeah... I know," he reluctantly acknowledged after a few moments.

"So how are you really doing?" Josh asked, hoping for the truth.

"I miss Tatiana big time."

"I figured as much, but that wasn't what I was really getting at."

"I know," Paco conceded. "Sometimes I miss the junk a little but since I wasn't shooting it, there wasn't any problem with withdrawals."

"Glad to hear that, and the booze?"

"Nothin. It was more of a social thing for me".

"You know once you get thru rehab you get to choose any path you want to take...Have you given it any thought?"

"I guess for the time being, I'm just concentrating on getting out of here."

"I think that's a great idea."

"I'm just so friggin bored. It is such a monotonous routine. Wake up, eat, go to therapy, eat, go to more therapy. It just keeps going and on and on."

"I know; that part's gotta suck. Maybe they are just trying to help you understand that you can have a good life without being all messed up."

"How the hell is this showing me I can have a good life?"

"Perhaps they're just trying to get you to think. You were given a brain for a reason, Paco."

"Is it too late to get a new one?"

"I'm afraid so," Josh said laughing to himself. "You are pretty much stuck with the one you've got. Have you ever heard the expression – garbage in, garbage out?"

"Huh?" Paco muttered in confusion.

"If," Josh elaborated, "all you do in put poison into your mind, how can you really expect anything worthwhile to come out of it? Just something for you to think about."

Josh glanced at his watch and added "I'd love to stay a bit longer but unfortunately I need to get going, I'm on my way to the courthouse."

"No worries, we've got group session at nine. I appreciate you stopping by."

"Oh, I almost forgot, your car's at your dads."

"Yeah, he told me." Paco offered up.

"Is there anything I can do for ya?"

"Did you find out about the community service?" Paco inquired, eager for some good news.

"What do they got you doing for chores around here?"

"It varies from day to day but it's mostly scrubbing the bathrooms or pushing a mop around. Maybe a couple of hours a day I guess."

"I think that we can get that to count. Leave that one up to me, okay."

When Paco failed to respond, Josh added, "I know it might not seem like it now, but I believe that one day you are going to look back and realize that everything you are going through is for a reason. Who knows, you might even come to understand that this ordeal may turn out to be the best thing that ever happened to you." With that, he gave him a hug goodbye and headed towards the door.

"Hey Josh", Paco called out to him.

"Yeah."

"Thanks again for not ratting me out. You were right, he wasn't that pissed."

"Happy to help little buddy, happy to help." With that, Josh meandered back to his car.

Josh met Clare & Adam in the lobby just outside the courtroom doors.

"Good morning, how are you doing today?"

"I'm a little nervous," Clare vocalized for the first time.

"Totally understandable," Josh said. "I just want you to relax, you have to trust that everything will work out okay."

"Sometimes it is easier said than done, Mr. Randall." Clare acknowledged.

"Did you get a chance to look over the questions I sent you?"

"It was mostly what I had expected," Clare affirmed, "but there were a few that bothered me."

Josh looked at her in a sympathetic manner. "Help me out here?"

"Do you really think," Clare barely whispered, "that his attorney will talk about sex?"

"I can almost guarantee it."

Clare shook her head in disbelief.

Josh tried his best to be sympathetic. "Because the plaintiff met privately with you to discuss different wedding cakes, more than likely, Clare, you will be the only one taking the stand. Nothing is etched in stone but if I were a gambling man..." Josh let the thought trial off. "I just want to remind you that if you are to be a credible witness, your testimony is going to have to be as truthful as possible. You don't need to hold anything back just to make yourself look better, okay."

"Okay," Clare echoed, as she wondered to herself why Josh would think it would be necessary for him to caution her about being truthful.

"I would like you to put me on the stand as well," Adam volunteered.

"If it comes to that, we definitely will," Josh said, in an accommodating fashion. "If you are ready, we should probably go inside."

Clare glanced over to the plaintiffs table. The first thing she noticed was how handsome Jeremy Mendoza, the attorney for the plaintiff, was. He looked as though he had stepped out of a magazine ad for Armani suits. She wanted to dislike him, but even she had to admit he looked extremely polished.

After the jury was brought in, the Judge announced that it was time for opening statements.

The attorney for the plaintiffs stood up. Clare immediately noticed that there wasn't a single wrinkle in his suit.

"Ladies and gentlemen of the jury," Jeremy started off, "I'd like to thank you for being here today. The reason why we are here is because on April 12, 2016 the defendants, Adam and Clare Robinson knowingly, and willfully chose to violate my client's civil rights."

He surveyed the courtroom and slowly made his way towards the jury box.

"A lot has changed since the founding of our country some two hundred and forty years ago. Thankfully, many things have changed for the better. The civil war helped to end slavery once and for all. The nineteenth amendment gave women the right to vote. And in 1964 congress passed the Civil Rights Act, which outlawed discrimination based on race, color, religion, sex, or national origin," Jeremy paused and carefully looked directly at each member of the jury for dramatic effect, "this law was later amended to include sexual orientation."

"My clients, in good faith, went to the establishment known as Heavenly Treats in Lakewood, Colorado to purchase a cake for their upcoming wedding. Keep in mind, that the defendants advertise on both their website, and also in the Denver Post, that one of their specialties is making wedding cakes."

"However," Jeremy continued, "once the defendants learned that this cake would be for a gay wedding, they decided that they no longer wished to conduct business with my clients. The reason why we are here today is to show the world that hatred will not be tolerated and it should not be considered acceptable behavior."

"I would like you to think about something for a moment," Jeremy added. "It was only fifty years ago that it was illegal for a black man to marry a white woman in this country. Less than forty years ago, in some states, men could be incarcerated for up to five years in prison for simply having consensual sex. Thankfully, we have progressed a great deal since then but there is still work to go. The plaintiffs are here today because they were refused service simply because they are gay. My clients are here to not only stand up for their civil rights, but they are also here to stand up for the civil rights of everyone, and to say that this kind of bigotry will no longer be tolerated in a civilized society. Thank you."

Jeremy deliberately walked as slowly as possible back to his table as if he was giving each member of the jury a few extra moments to savor his thought provoking words.

When the attorney for the plaintiffs had finished with his opening remarks, Justice Hayden politely announced that the defense may now present their opening statement.

Josh looked over at the jury and rose out of his chair in a leisurely manner. For dramatic effect, he picked off an imaginary piece of lint from the sleeve of his suit jacket. Then, after a lengthy pause he gently tapped his upper lip and thoughtfully said...

"Good Morning ladies and gentlemen. I too, would like to thank you all for coming here and exercising your civic duties. I feel I must start this off by apologizing due to the fact that today we are literally going to tackle two very difficult topics – politics and religion. I'm glad the plaintiffs decided to bring up the founding of our nation because the laws that govern this great country are actually based upon Judeo-Christian principles."

Josh nonchalantly walked back over to the defendant's table and picked up a copy of the Constitution. "The U.S. Constitution," Josh continued as he held the copy in his hand, "Such an amazing document. Our forefathers were so insightful, they understood the nature of freewill, and they also knew that with God's help, it was our destiny that we should be able to govern ourselves."

Josh walked back to the defendant's table and gently placed the copy on his desk, and then proceeded to pick up what looked like another ancient manuscript. "Up until the very point when Thomas Jefferson penned the Declaration of Independence, people were told that our rights came from our rulers." Josh then proceeded to recite it from memory. "We hold these truths to be self-evident that all men are created equal, that they are endowed by their Creator with certain unalienable rights that among these are Life, Liberty and the pursuit of Happiness."

"It was no accident that Thomas Jefferson chose to use the phrase endowed by their Creator." Josh repeated it again for dramatic effect. "Endowed by their Creator."

"Despite what many politicians might like you to believe, our founding fathers understood that these unalienable rights do not come from government, but instead they come from God. They were so adamant about this, that they would not ratify the Constitution without the Bill of Rights. And the very first amendment in the Bill of Rights – Congress shall make no law respecting an establishment of religion, or prohibiting the free exercise thereof;"

"It is the prohibiting the free exercise thereof that we will be focusing upon today."

"The plaintiffs will argue that my clients refused to make them a cake because it was for a gay wedding. We are not disputing this fact. We are not here to dispute the fact that my client's actions may have offended the plaintiffs. We are even willing to concede that my client's actions may have caused the plaintiffs some sort of emotional distress."

Josh looked over toward the table where the plaintiffs were sitting.

"My clients did not refuse to serve the defendants because of their lifestyle. They never told him that he wasn't welcome in their store. They politely informed the plaintiff, Mr. Thomas Addicott, that because of their religious beliefs, they did not feel comfortable making a cake for a gay wedding."

"My clients are sitting before you today, because they believe in God. They believe that there is such a thing as "right" and "wrong" and that these laws do not come from the government but from a higher power.

They understand that we all will be held accountable for what we do in this lifetime, and that the choices we make in this lifetime will determine how we spend eternity."

"What we have here today is a set of two equally significant laws. On the one hand you have the plaintiffs saying that my clients violated their civil rights and on the other hand, you have the defendants arguing that the first amendment guarantees them the right to practice their faith as they see fit. The question put forth to you today is, what happens when you have two valid and important laws that seemingly contradict one another?"

"It all comes down to beliefs. The plaintiffs believe their personal desires are more important than the defendant's belief in God. Once you hear all the evidence, you get to decide for yourselves what rings true."

Yet again, Josh paused for dramatic effect and took the time to look at each and every jury member directly in the eyes.

"Thank you so very much for your time."

Both Clare and Adam smiled at each other and relaxed as they were now feeling a bit more comfortable with their decision to use Josh as their attorney.

many are called

The judge announced "The plaintiffs may call their first witness."

"Thank you, your honor," Jeremy calmly stood up and said, "at this time the plaintiffs would like to call Mrs. Elizabeth Clare Robinson to the stand."

Josh leaned his head in towards Clare and encouragingly whispered, "You've got this; everything is going to be fine."

Clare involuntarily swallowed the nonexistent bile she perceived to be rising up in her throat and silently prayed to herself. "Lord, please grant me the strength and wisdom to find the right words so that I might glorify you. Amen"

As she walked towards the witness stand, it was almost as if time seemed to stand still. In this imaginary state of suspended animation, a range of different emotions flooded her mind. Confidence... Anxiety... Fear... Trepidation. She tried to remember what her Pilates instructor told her about breathing from your diaphragm. She gazed at the judge, looked over at the members of the jury and then back at the empty witness stand. She wondered if this is what it felt like when a prisoner was being walked to the gallows. She shook her head ever so slightly as if to knock that last thought out of her brain.

The bailiff stopped Clare in her tracks. He held out a Bible.

Clare placed her left hand on the worn, leather bound copy. It felt warm and comforting to the touch.

"Please raise your right hand. Do you swear to tell the truth, the whole truth and nothing but the truth?"

A surge of adrenalin went through her mind. For the first time in her life she was being asked to take an actual oath to God in regards to her honesty. On an intellectual level, Clare understood that God had the capacity to see everything, but now it was somehow different. It almost felt like her entire life was being placed under a microscope and God was able to examine every single lie she had told when she was a little girl.

The judge interrupted her train of thought. "Would you please answer the bailiff?"

Clare was jolted back to reality. "I do."

"You may take the stand."

"Good morning, how are you doing today?" The attorney asked her in a very polite and sincere tone.

Clare leaned in to the microphone. "I am fine, thank you." He seemed not only polished but very courteous as well, she thought to herself.

"For the record would you please state your full name?"

"My name is Elizabeth Clare Robinson."

"And would you please tell this court what you do for a living."

"I" Clare immediately corrected herself, "my husband and I, own Heavenly Treats bakery."

"Fantastic. And how long have you been in business?"

"We opened our doors almost nine years ago."

"So your business is open to the public?"

"Of course, who else would we be serving?"

A few members of the jury silently chuckled at Clare's response to the absurdity of the question.

"Is there any special criteria needed to become a customer?"

"I suppose you have to like pastries."

Some of the jurors snickered in unison.

Where was this coming from? Clare wondered to herself. She was never sarcastic nor had she ever tried to be intentionally funny.

"So anyone is welcome in your store?"

"Yes," she answered politely.

"Do you remember the events which took place on April 12th 2016?"

"Not down to the very last detail." Clare responded as truthfully as possible.

"But you do remember my client, Mr. Thomas Addicott coming into your shop?"

"Of course."

"And could you please tell the jury exactly why he was there."

"I believe he bought some baked goods, but I suppose the main reason why he came in that day, was to order a wedding cake."

Jeremy paused in mid thought. "I'd like to back up for a moment. You said that day. Had my client been in your bakery before?"

"I can't say with absolute certainty, but I believe so."

"Are you insinuating that my client was a regular patron?"

"I wouldn't go so far as to say regular." Clare paused to make certain that she was being absolutely truthful. "We have some customers that come in on almost a daily basis, but I think I can safely say that he had been in there before."

"Just for the record," Jeremy sought clarification, "you don't think my client frequented your establishment enough for you to know him as a regular customer."

Clare leaned into the microphone "That's correct."

"Did my client immediately ask about enlisting your services to make a wedding cake?"

"Not at first, I believe he was actually looking at pastries when he first came into the shop."

"But at some point, my client did ask you about making a wedding cake?"

"That's correct," Clare answered. "Since we were not that busy, I invited Mr. Addicott to come into our back office where we keep our wedding portfolio album."

"And what might that be?"

"It's just a photo album with pictures of some of the different wedding cakes we have made over the years. Sometimes it helps the customer if they can see actual images instead of having to describe to us what they have in their mind."

"I see. And at this point was there any animosity between yourself and my client, Mr. Addicott?"

"There was never any animosity and there still isn't now." Clare looked over at the plaintiffs table and gave Thomas a very warm and genuine smile.

Thomas did his best to look stoic.

"But at some point, things changed?" Jeremy said in a probing manner.

"I don't think so," Clare responded truthfully.

Jeremy held up his finger. "Yes, but there came a time where you no longer wished to serve my client. Is that correct?"

"I no longer wished to make him a wedding cake if that is what you are asking?" Clare verified.

"Yes, that is what I was asking,"

"Did Mr. Addicott announce that he wanted you to make a cake for a gay wedding?"

"I don't recall him using those exact words."

"So, you just arbitrarily decided that he was no longer worthy of your services?"

"I never said that. I believe I told him that I simply did not feel comfortable making a cake for a gay wedding."

"Did my client volunteer that he was gay?"

"No, he did not, at least not at first."

"Then what made you change your mind? Do you normally go around assessing whether or not someone is gay?"

"No, of course not," Clare said in a curt tone.

"So why would you decide to refuse his business?"

"I think when he started talking about his partner, the alarm bells went off."

There was a slight twinkle in Jeremy's eye when he heard the phrase "alarm bells" but he would save that for later.

"If I am understanding you correctly, my client never came into your shop and announced that he wanted you to make a cake for a gay wedding?"

"That's correct. I think it was when he said something about Ethan will love this: that I knew for sure."

"And it was at this point that you told him you no longer wanted his business?" Jeremy goaded her.

"No," Clare corrected him. "I simply told him that I really didn't feel comfortable making a cake for a gay wedding."

"And why is that Mrs. Robinson?"

Clare looked over towards Josh hoping to get any subtle indication as to how she should continue. When she perceived a slight nod, Clare understood that it was acceptable to give her desired answer.

"Because I believe that marriage is supposed to be between a man and a woman."

"Do you believe in God, Mrs. Robinson?"

"Absolutely," she said, as she smiled to herself at the thought.

"And you have been a Christian all your life?"

"Since High School."

"Once you decided to become a Christian, did you immediately know everything there was to know about the religion?" Jeremy asked in an inquisitive manner.

"No."

"Is it safe to say you know more today than you did ten or fifteen years ago?"

"That's correct."

"Have you ever been wrong Mrs. Robinson?"

Clare was taken aback with his insinuation.

"Please answer the question. Have you ever been wrong?"

"Yes, of course I've been wrong before."

"So," Jeremy continued, "there have been times in your life where you can look back and see that there was something you may have said, or maybe even done, that was wrong?"

"Yes."

"Do you enjoy sex Mrs. Robinson?"

Clare immediately recoiled as though someone had thrown a bucket of ice water in her face.

"Excuse me?" were the only words she could muster.

Josh tried to save her, "Objection Your Honor – Relevance?" but it was too late.

Finally, Clare thought to herself, it is about time Josh came to her rescue.

"Your Honor," Jeremy pleaded, "I would ask the court's permission for a little leeway on this as to the fact my clients were discriminated on the basis of their sexual orientation."

The judge looked over at Jeremy and said in a stern voice. "I am going to allow it, but I am warning you Mr. Mendoza, this is a courtroom so please tread lightly. Overruled."

"Thank you, your honor."

Justice Paul Hayden was a stout, no nonsense type of man who took his oath of impartiality almost as seriously as he did his sacred marriage vows. After twenty years as a district attorney he was finally awarded a judgeship. He was entrusted to rule over this courtroom and he refused to tolerate any preposterous or unethical behavior.

He turned towards Clare and with the most sympathetic eyes. "Please answer the question."

Clare let out an exaggerated sigh, glanced over at Adam as if she might be able to draw upon his inner strength and finally said, "I do."

"Is it safe to say that most people would describe sex as pleasurable?" Jeremy encouraged.

"I cannot speak for most people," Clare said, "but if you are asking if I think sex is pleasurable, the answer is yes."

Josh was quietly smiling to himself, as he was happy to see that Clare had regained her composure and was holding her own.

Jeremy resumed his interrogation of the witness "Just as some people prefer chocolate and others prefer vanilla..."

Josh knew exactly where he was going with this, "Objection your Honor- Relevance?"

Justice Hayden held up his finger as if to momentarily pause the situation: "I am going to allow it, but once again, I am warning you Mr. Mendoza this is a courtroom. Overruled."

"I understand, your honor." Jeremy paused a few extra seconds to find the exact words he was looking for. "I'm fairly certain that you do realize that with over six billion people on this planet, no two people are going to have the exact same tastes."

"Objection – Argumentative." Josh said, hoping to help change the subject.

Before Justice Hayden could say anything, Jeremy offered up, "Let me rephrase that. Do you understand that the term sex can be used to cover a multitude of different, how can I put this delicately – acts?"

"Yes," Clare said with a sigh, as she tried her best not to visualize what he was saying.

"Previously you told this courtroom that you believe in God, is that correct?"

"Yes," Clare said in a relieved tone happy to be on a more comfortable subject.

"And you believe that God will forgive you for your sins?"

"Only if you ask Him," Clare confirmed.

Jeremy then asked "Is there any sin that is unforgiveable?"

Clare paused and thought about it momentarily, then said "No."

"So," Jeremy continued, "I could murder someone and God would forgive me?"

"If you asked for forgiveness," Clare said, correcting him.

"Does that also include stealing and lying?"

"I believe that God is willing to forgive you for any possible sin, as long as you ask." Clare volunteered.

"So," Jeremy said, as he looked at the judge with trepidation, "God would be willing to forgive you even if you indulged in a lesbian relationship?"

"Yes, as long as..."

Jeremy cut her off mid-sentence. "Thank you, that will be all for now."

Clare started to say ..."but."

Jeremy reiterated, "That will be all for now. I have no more questions for this witness."

Justice Hayden jumped right in. "Normally at this time the defense would be given the opportunity to cross examine the witness." He looked up at the clock and noticed that it was rapidly approaching noon. "However," he continued, "I think this would be a good time to break for lunch."

Looking over at the jury, Justice Hayden continued to inform them... "They have an excellent cafeteria down on the basement floor. It's a little pricy, but the food is actually quite good. I want to remind you, you are not to discuss this case with each other, and because this is a highly publicized case, I would ask you to please refrain from using the internet or any other form of social media. Are we clear on that?"

The members of the jury nodded in agreement.

"I think if we had everyone back here at 1:30 that should give us plenty of time."

Like clockwork, the bailiff stood up and said "All rise."

a sign of the times

As soon as they were in the hallway Josh said, "Follow me. I don't think we should use the front entrance. It looks like there is starting to be quite a crowd outside."

They quietly slipped out a side exit which spilled directly onto the sidewalk. "There is a great little restaurant kitty corner from here," Josh informed them.

As Adam, Clare and Josh headed toward the diner, Clare chewed on the inside of her lower lip as she walked. She couldn't stop wondering why Josh had let the questioning spin out of control. Why didn't he step in? Why didn't he come to her rescue? There were a million questions she wanted to ask when the right moment came.

Thankfully, they successfully managed the trek without anyone from the gathering crowd noticing who they were.

Once they were safely in the confines of the restaurant, the hostess offered them a table directly in front of the window where they could witness the ensuing scene.

"How come there are so many people?" Adam asked, as though he were unaware of the trial.

In the grassy park directly across the street from the courthouse, a large crowd had gathered. Some carrying rainbow flags, some had picket signs. It looked as though they were being taunted by a smaller group of maybe fifteen to twenty people. One of the men doing the shouting, was holding up a sign that read God Hates Fags.

Adam looked out the window and silently wondered if there was anyone who seriously thought that those bigots from the Westboro Baptist Church really represented Christianity.

"In case you haven't noticed," Josh offered, "this is now ground zero for the gay rights movement. They see you as a symbol of religious intolerance."

"How could they think that?" said Clare, truly wondering why.

"It's actually quite understandable," Josh theorized. "Hollywood and the progressive media control most of the information people get and if someone has the audacity to view the world differently, they are often portrayed as bigoted and intolerant. You guys might not like to hear this, but a large portion of the population has been brainwashed into thinking that Christians are the enemy."

"Why on earth would we be the enemy?" Adam asked, as if this was some sort of alien concept.

"Sometimes the truth is a scary thing. Let's just say for the time being that Christians are portrayed in a less than flattering light. Since you are Christians, and you're standing up for your values, they view you as a threat. Sorry to tell you this but it's probably going to get a lot worse before it gets better."

"Terrific," Clare mumbled to herself.

"Unfortunately, we don't have an unlimited amount of time today so we should probably get our order in as soon as possible," Josh said in a helpful tone.

After taking everyone's order, the waitress volunteered, "I'll be right back with your drinks."

Clare did her best to patiently wait for the waitress to finish. No sooner had she left the table she blurted out...

"How come you didn't object? How come you didn't demand that I should be allowed to finish my thought process? I should have been allowed to let the jury know that God would forgive them as long as they repented."

Josh sat silently as he let Clare vent. "Take a deep breath. Do you have everything out of your system?"

Clare nodded.

"Remember," Josh said, trying to slow down the pace of the conversation, "when I told you that the job of the plaintiff's attorney was to discredit you?"

"Yes."

"Well you held your own today: and you did good. He was simply doing his job."

"But why didn't he let me finish?" Clare asked.

"He wants to control the conversation, sometimes it is important to pick and choose your battles. I want you to think of this as a boxing match, even though they may not be aware of it, we are in control of this fight. Our goal is to convince members of the jury, the people hearing all the evidence, that your side of the argument makes more sense. The only thing I can say is that is a step by step process."

"I pray to God you know what you are doing." Clare said, as she slowly shook her head.

"Me too." Josh said aloud and silently mumbled it again to himself.

They did their best to keep the remainder of the conversation light hearted while enjoying their lunch.

stand firm in the faith

After they arrived back in the courtroom, Clare took her seat in the witness stand.

Once the judge was seated, he looked over at Clare and said "I want to remind you, you are still under oath."

"I understand" Clare acknowledged.

"Would the defense like to cross examine this witness?"

"Yes, your honor," Josh said as he was rising from his chair.

Josh understood that he was now on center stage. He slowly rose from his seat, straightened his red striped tie that Susan had picked out for him and slowly walked towards the witness stand.

"Good Afternoon Mrs. Robinson. How are you holding up? Can I get you some water?"

"No, I am fine, thank you," Clare revealed, and she meant it.

"Great. Do you understand why we are here today?"

"Of course!" Clare said, as she anxiously waited to present her side of the story. "The plaintiffs feel that we somehow infringed on their civil rights."

"Just so we make everything perfectly clear for the jury, you did refuse to make a wedding cake for the plaintiffs?" Josh stated in the form of a question.

"Yes."

"So this is a fact that is not in dispute."

"That's correct."

"Was your refusal in any way meant to hurt or humiliate the plaintiffs?"

"No, of course not," Clare said truthfully.

"Mrs. Robinson, do you have any signs in your establishment saying no blacks allowed?"

"Of course not." She repeated, looking a little shocked. She never expected that Josh would ask such an offensive question.

"Is there anything on the door that prohibits say, Mexicans or Jews or Muslims from entering your shop?"

"Absolutely not," Clare affirmed, but she still wasn't sure where he was taking this.

"How about gays?"

"No." she said with a heavy sigh.

"Did you ever tell Mr. Addicott that he was no longer welcome in your shop?"

"No."

"Did you refuse to serve him because he was gay?"

"No, I simply informed him that I did not feel comfortable making a cake for a gay wedding,"

"And why is that?"

"Objection - Speculation" Jeremy said trying to insert his will back into the conversation.

"Overruled," declared Justice Hayden. "I will allow it. You may answer the question."

"I believe that a marriage is supposed to be between a man and a woman," Clare said with an air of conviction.

"Why would you say such a thing?" Josh asked with feigned outrage.

Clare gave him a bewildered look. She wasn't certain if Josh wanted her to mention the scriptures or not.

Josh nodded his head slightly and gave her a pleading look to let her know it was okay.

"Because it says so in the Bible."

Josh nodded in agreement and gave her a discrete little smile. "So what you are trying to tell this courtroom is that you turned down business because of something you read in a book?"

Not just any book," Clare stipulated, "I believe the bible to be the word of God?"

"The Word of God?" Josh repeated, in an almost mocking tone. "Are you trying to tell this courtroom that you believe God sat down and handwrote every word in the bible?"

"I think it was inspired by God. I believe that God uses the Bible to communicate directly with us and at the very same time it helps to give us a better understanding of His nature."

"How could God possibly use something so simple as a book to communicate with human beings? You have to admit, that this sounds a bit far-fetched."

"To me, it makes perfect sense. If you were to imagine a God powerful enough to create the entire universe in the blink of an eye, doesn't it seem plausible that He is capable of doing anything? Even using written words to reach across time and space and speak directly with His creation. I realize that a lot of people this may find this difficult to swallow but I can assure you that the more you read, the more you will understand." Clare proclaimed to the jury.

"That's a very interesting way of looking at it." Josh affirmed. "Let me switch subjects for a moment. How much do wedding cakes usually cost?"

"Anywhere from four hundred to a fifteen hundred dollars," Clare divulged honestly.

"For a cake?" Josh mused with absolute astonishment.

"There is a lot of work involved..."

"Okay." Josh said interrupting. "That sounds like a substantial amount of money to turn down."

Clare thought about it for a moment. "It is, but it isn't about the money. We feel it is more important to serve the Lord."

"And you feel that you were doing God's will by refusing to bake a cake?" Josh inquired as if he were completely puzzled by the prospect.

"I feel that we are called to obey God's word and it clearly states that a marriage is between a man and a woman."

"Remember when my distinguished colleague Mr. Mendoza," Josh pointed over to the attorney sitting at plaintiff's table, "asked if you knew more about Christianity today than you did ten or fifteen years ago?"

"Yes."

"Is it possible that you might be able to comprehend the nature of God a little bit better fifty years from now?"

"If I have the good fortune of living that long, I'd certainly like to think so."

"I like that answer." Josh thought to himself... now might be a good time to plant a seed or two.

"Can God do anything He wants?"

"I believe God can do whatever He chooses so long as it does not contradict His holy and pure nature."

"I'm not sure I'm following you. Would you please elaborate for the courtroom."

"Well," said Clare, "the way I understand it, since God is unconditionally perfect, He is incapable of doing anything that is deceitful or dishonest."

"Thank you for the clarification. But if God decided to, couldn't He use anyone, even someone who is deeply flawed, to help others understand the truth?"

Clare took a few seconds to mull over what Josh was saying and politely responded. "Absolutely, the bible is filled with examples of God utilizing imperfect people to help advance His message."

As soon as Josh was about to dismiss Clare from the witness stand, another random thought popped into his mind. "I'm sorry one last question. Once you realized that the plaintiff was gay, did you ask him to immediately leave the property?"

"Of course not."

"Thank you for your testimony. No further questions at this time."

Jeremy rose slightly from his chair. "Redirect, your Honor."

Jeremy approached the witness stand.

"If someone wants to purchase a wedding cake for a friend or a family member, is it allowed?"

"I'm not sure I follow you?"

"Let's say my daughter is getting married and I want to surprise her by ordering a wedding cake, would I be able to buy a cake for her, from your establishment?"

"Of course."

"You had mentioned earlier that when my client said and I quote - Ethan would love this one, you said that alarm bells went off. Was there a fire in your building?"

"No, it was simply an expression," Clare responded in annoyance.

"So up until that point you did not know my client was gay."

"I did not, nothing in his mannerisms gave any indication he was gay."

"I'm sorry, could you repeat that. Did you say nothing in his mannerisms?"

"Those were my words," Clare reassured him.

"And at any point did my client come out and say that he was gay?"

"I don't recall him ever phrasing it that way, but he confirmed my suspicions when he told me his parents still weren't completely comfortable with the idea either."

"You don't like homosexuals or lesbians, do you Mrs. Robinson?"

"Objection- Inflammatory" said Josh, hoping to save Clare from further embarrassment.

"Sustained"

"Let me rephrase that question. Does my client's lifestyle make you uncomfortable?" Jeremy asked.

"Yes," Clare replied truthfully.

"Do you have any gay friends Mrs. Robinson?"

"Objection – Relevance," said Josh.

"It goes to show the defendant's character." Jeremy quipped.

"I will allow it." Justice Hayden said.

"No, I do not," said Clare succinctly.

"Not a niece, a nephew, no cousins, friends of the family?" prodded Jeremy.

"Not to my knowledge."

"It seems a little bit strange to me, given the statistics... say anywhere between five and ten percent of the population consider themselves to be gay. Maybe they are afraid to confide in you, for fear of how you might react."

Josh started to rise from his seat.

"It's okay you don't need to answer that," Jeremy said, as he held up his hand. "I withdraw the question. At this time there are no further questions for this witness your honor."

"Would the council for the defense like to redirect?"

Josh rose slightly from his chair, "not at this time your honor."

"You are free to step down," Justice Hayden informed her.

Clare's head was spinning from that last go round. She felt as though she was on the losing end of a heavyweight fight. She felt a little irritated that Josh did not allow her a chance to explain herself. How could he not object she wondered? As she plunked herself into her chair next to Adam, Josh whispered in her ear. "You did great: this will all make sense later."

Once Clare was seated back at the defendants table, Justice Hayden said, "You may call your next witness."

Jeremy rose slightly and said "At this time the plaintiffs would like to call Mr. Thomas Addicott to the stand."

After being sworn in, Thomas took his seat in the witness box.

"Would you state your name for the record?" Jeremy inquired in such a manner as to hint to the jury that they had just met.

"Thomas Michael Addicott."

"And what do you do for a living Mr. Addicott?"

"I'm physical therapist," Thomas answered truthfully.

"How nice," Jeremy said, "I imagine that it is a very rewarding career."

"It's fulfilling. It is nice to know that what you are doing can make a difference in someone's life." Thomas proclaimed, as he looked over towards the jury.

"I couldn't agree more. I realize that this may be painful for you but if you could, would you please tell the members of the jury what happened on the morning of April 12, 2016."

"Sure, well my partner...Ethan," Thomas gave him a discrete little wave with his pinky, "and I had recently gotten engaged and we were starting to make arrangements for our wedding."

"How exciting," Jeremy gleefully added, then he looked around and sheepishly realized that he probably shouldn't be interrupting the testimony. "I'm sorry, please continue."

"In addition to all the usual arrangements such as picking out a venue, flowers, catering...we also needed a wedding cake."

"But your wedding is not until August?"

"We didn't want to wait until the very last moment."

"I understand. Please continue."

"I believe it was a Tuesday," Thomas correctly recalled. "Since I wasn't working that day, I decided to tackle that project myself. I starting off by doing a Google search for wedding cakes, and several different local bakeries popped up."

"And Heavenly Treats was one of the bakeries?" Jeremy asked in an encouraging tone.

"That's correct," Thomas verified. "As soon as I saw the name, I immediately knew the shop, because we had been there before. It's actually not that far from Ethan's office. Anyway, it was around 11:00-ish when I stopped by. I think that there were maybe two or three people ahead of me so I went over to the glass case to see if there was something I could pick up for dessert. When it was my turn to be helped: the owner, Mrs. Robinson," Thomas pointed toward Clare for good measure, "invited me into the back to look at pictures of some of the different wedding cakes they made."

"And did you find one that you liked?"

"When I picked out a cake that I thought Ethan would love, that was when she got all weird."

"What do you mean by weird?" Jeremy inquired trying to help the story along.

"Well, she was originally so polite and helpful when I first told her I wanted to purchase a wedding cake. I guess it was because she probably was thinking about all the profits she would be making. However, when I mentioned my partner Ethan, something about her demeanor changed. It was almost as if she wanted nothing to do with me."

"Did she throw you out?" Jeremy asked in disbelief.

"No, nothing that dramatic," Thomas said, "but I could sense an awkward tension."

"And then what happened?"

"She told me that she didn't feel comfortable making a wedding cake for a gay couple."

"I'm so sorry" Jeremy consoled him as if, just talking about the horrific ordeal was traumatizing his very soul. "Please continue."

"I did my best to put on a brave face, I didn't want to give her the satisfaction of letting her know how much she had hurt me."

Clare looked horrified as she listened to his account of the story.

"I wanted to be stoic. I did not want to let her see how torn up I was." As he choked back the tears, Thomas took a deep breath and continued his version of the events. "It's just hard to imagine how some people can be so insensitive."

"So, did she tell you to leave her store?"

"No, I think to appease her guilty conscience she looked up the names of several different bakeries in the area that also made wedding cakes."

"And then what did you do?" Jeremy asked in mock exaggeration.

"I decided to take the high road, I didn't say anything rude and I even bought a few pastries just so she couldn't be upset with me for wasting any of her precious time."

"That was a nice gesture," Jeremy offered.

"I try to be nice whenever possible," Thomas explained as he looked to the jury to find anyone who might be sympathetic to his plight.

"And then what happened?"

"I tried my best to forget about the entire incident but the more I thought about it, the more it bothered me. I couldn't sleep at night. It was hard for me to focus on my job. This is 2016, why does there have to be such hatred in this world?"

"I couldn't agree more," said Jeremy. "No further questions at this time."

"I think this would be a good time to wrap things up for the day." Looking over at the jury Justice Mendoza added, "I want to remind you, you are not to discuss this case with anyone, husbands, wives, children – anyone. As I had mentioned earlier please refrain from using any social media for the time being. This is a highly publicized case so please, no watching the news either. See you all here tomorrow 9am sharp."

The bailiff stood up and politely said, "All rise." Once everyone was standing, the judge thanked the courtroom and retreated back to his chambers.

Clare held her tongue until they had exited the courtroom. Once they were in the hall, she pulled Josh aside. "How come you didn't object? How could you let him say those things?"

"Clare," Josh said, "Remember when I told you how it would probably be a bad idea if I came into your shop and told you how to make pastries?"

"Yes."

"Well, I want you to think of this courtroom as my bakery. I know what I am doing here. First off, the odds are that almost every single person on that jury knows someone who is gay. Second, the plaintiffs are already trying to make you look like the bad guy. We do not need to be the antagonists here. Besides, can you say with absolute certainty, that the plaintiff wasn't upset on the inside when you told him your feelings?"

"No," Clare said honestly.

"You have to give him the benefit of the doubt here. Nothing is spinning out of control. But this is a process. Now I want you both to go home and relax." Josh said in a comforting tone. "This isn't over but you've already gotten through the hardest part."

"Are you going to put me on the stand tomorrow?" Adam asked, hoping to be able to contribute.

"Right now, it is the plaintiffs turn to present their side of the argument. Once they have finished, then it will be our opportunity. At this point, I'm still not sure."

"But I really would like the chance to explain my beliefs to the jury." Adam stressed, trying to be as helpful as possible.

"I am well aware. For the time being, I am concentrating on taking things day by day. Try to think of it as a chess match, we need to see what they are going to do, before we plan our next move. Fair enough?"

"Fair enough," Adam repeated back to him.

with humility comes wisdom

The next morning Josh called Adam to say he was running a bit late, so they agreed to meet inside the courtroom instead of out in the hall. After everyone had returned to their respective seats, the bailiff walked Thomas back to the witness stand.

"I want to remind you Mr. Addicott," Justice Hayden said "you are still under oath."

"Would the defense like to cross examine the witness?"

Josh let out a deep sigh, adjusted his tie for good measure and slowly walked towards the witness stand.

"Good Morning Mr. Addicott, how are you doing today?"

"Fine," said Thomas trying to do exactly as his attorney instructed, keeping his answers brief.

"Are you well rested?" Josh asked in earnest.

"Yes."

"That's great news," said Josh "I'm sure the jury will be happy to hear that you are no longer troubled by sleepless nights."

Thomas' face reddened ever so slightly as he realized that Josh had caught him in a lie. He hoped the jury didn't notice.

"How are the wedding plans coming along?"

"Everything is going well, thank you for asking." Thomas said, politely.

"Good. I'm glad to hear that. Getting back to the day in question, when Mrs. Robinson suggested that she did not feel comfortable making a cake for a gay wedding, you had mentioned to her that your parents had also expressed some discomfort about the situation – is that correct?"

"That's correct. I suppose in the beginning my parents were a little uncomfortable... but now they are fine with it. They just want me to be happy." Thomas added.

"That's fantastic. Everybody deserves a chance to be happy." Josh said in a most agreeable manner.

"Did Mrs. Robinson use any language which might cause you to think she hated gay people?"

"Not that I can recall," said Thomas.

"No homophobic slurs of any kind?"

"No."

"Were you upset when you found out the defendants were Christians?"

"No, it doesn't really bother me." Thomas answered truthfully.

"But you don't believe in God yourself?" Josh speculated.

"Objection – Relevance," Jeremy argued, as he rose slightly from his chair.

Josh continued, "Your honor, since my clients are on trial because of their beliefs, what the plaintiff does or does not believe is directly relevant."

"I'm going to allow it. Overruled."

"Okay," Josh continued. "You don't believe in God, do you?

"No, I do not. I like to believe in facts."

"I see," Josh said, as he contemplated his next move. "It seems to me that you have a scientific mind."

"Let's say logical," Thomas corrected him.

"My bad, so is it safe to say you don't really believe in things that cannot be proven?"

"Yes."

"Do you believe in love, Mr. Addicott?"

Thomas looked over at Ethan, tilted his head slightly and gave him a loving smile. "Very much so."

"That seems highly illogical. Love doesn't seem to be very scientific. Love can't be seen, Love can't be held ... Love can't be measured; there is really no way that you can actually quantify love – yet despite your logical mind, you are willing to concede that love exists?"

"Yes I am, but love can actually be explained by evolution," said Thomas trying to justify his beliefs.

"How so?"

"Love is an evolutionary trait. We have evolved to want to nourish one another, sort of a bonding process."

"I see," Josh said thoughtfully. "But how does that explain hate? Are those who hate, simply lower on the evolutionary scale?"

Josh held up his hand stopping him from giving a reply. "You don't need to answer that. So is it safe to assume that you believe in evolution?"

"All the evidence seems to prove that that is the case."

"I think I read somewhere that scientists claim the earth is about four and a half billion years old." Josh speculated. "Is that about right?"

"I suppose so," Thomas acknowledged.

"And you believe that over millions and millions of years we have evolved from simple amoeba to all the way up to the human beings we see here today?"

"I would be inclined to agree," Thomas said, as he leaned into the microphone.

"Are you willing to concede that if you go back far enough into our evolutionary past, on some distant level that all human beings must be related to one another?"

"That sounds reasonable."

"Great, I'm happy this is something we can agree upon. And for the record, you had mentioned that you don't believe in God? Why is that?"

"I think it is kind of foolish to believe in a magical being that will make all your wishes come true once you die."

"When you put it that way," Josh said with a smile, "it sounds very suspicious to me too."

A few members of the jury smiled at Josh's willingness to acknowledge the absurdity of the argument.

"Just to clarify things a bit," Josh restated the obvious, "you do believe you will eventually die?"

Thomas wanted to say "Duh" but he shook his head softly and said, "Yes I understand that I will eventually die"

"Sorry about that, I wasn't trying to make fun of you, but sometimes people don't like to think about death. I suspect if I were talking to a teenager, they might think of dying as something that just happens to old people."

"It's okay." Thomas said in a reassuring tone. "I understand."

"And what do you think happens when we die?" Josh asked.

"Nothing."

"Nothing?" Josh repeated the word as though he could not believe what he was hearing.

"I think once you die," Thomas offered, "your brain waves cease to exist and there are no more thoughts."

"If there is absolutely nothing more," Josh said thoughtfully, "that means this life is not a dress-rehearsal."

"Yes, I believe that this life is all we get."

"So, given the fact that we are only here for a relatively short period, wouldn't you say it was prudent to make the most of your time here on earth?"

"Of course."

"Is it safe to assume you would be an advocate of people doing what makes them happy?"

"Yes."

"Are you in agreement that if someone enjoyed eating chocolate cake and wanted to eat it three times a day, seven days a week, they should be able to do so, right?"

"If that is what they want to do," Thomas said, but then thought about it momentarily and added, "although they would have to understand that certain actions may have negative ramifications. If someone were to eat nothing but chocolate cake, they might develop health problems such as diabetes, or tooth decay."

"Now I think I am beginning to understand your beliefs. Everyone should be able to live their life exactly as they want but they should know that some of their choices may have consequences."

"Exactly."

"So, if I wanted to rob a bank," Josh continued to take the conversation to its extreme, "I have to understand that there may be serious repercussions if I get caught."

"I'd like to clarify," Thomas replied. "I didn't mean to say that people should be able to do anything they want."

"And why not?" Josh said with amazement.

"As a civilized society, we have enacted certain laws to protect people from the harmful behaviors of others."

"Why should that matter?" Josh inquired, not knowing what to make of these new rules.

"As man has evolved from small hunter/gatherer groups into more complex societies, certain restraints are necessary to ensure that people can live in harmony." Thomas said in a thought-provoking way.

"I think I am following you," Josh proclaimed. "I am guessing you would argue that we should be able to live our lives exactly as we choose so long as it does not hurt or infringe on others."

"Yes," Thomas declared, nodding in agreement.

"That makes perfect sense," Josh acknowledged as if he was finally learning about the truth for the very first time. "Let me ask you, if a society had enacted an unjust law, would you feel compelled to follow it?"

"I'm not sure I understand."

"Let me give you an example," Josh volunteered. "Have you ever heard of the Fugitive Slave Act of 1850?"

"I'm not familiar with it," Thomas revealed, with all sincerity.

"I'm paraphrasing this a bit, but the law basically required that all runaway slaves, if they were captured, were to be returned back to their rightful owners. In addition, all government and local officials including citizens of Free states, were mandated to cooperate with this law."

"I wasn't aware," Thomas replied, looking a bit horrified at the thought of it.

"That's okay, it was a very long time ago," Josh reassured him. "Do you think that it would have been more important for people to follow their conscience and help runaway slaves to escape, or follow the unjust law set forth by the government?"

"One should never be forced to follow an unjust law." Thomas readily agreed.

"I'm sorry," Josh said, "I didn't quite hear you. Could you repeat that for the jury?"

"I said you should never be forced to follow an unjust law."

Clare was smiling ear to ear.

"Thank you," said Josh and he added almost as if it was an afterthought, "do you remember when you first took the stand, you took an oath to tell the truth?"

"I do," said Thomas as he began to wonder where this was going,

"Do you believe in the truth?" Josh asked in an inquisitive manner.

"I think that truth is a personal thing. What is true for me may not be true for you," said Thomas, hoping his explanation helped to clarify his beliefs.

"Ok, so let me see if I understand you," said Josh. "You feel that everyone is entitled to their beliefs and as long as it is true for them, it counts as truth."

"I've never really tried to analyze it: but I think it is something like that."

"I'm just trying to understand things from your perspective. You are sitting here in this courtroom because you believe that the defendants have discriminated against you and your partner is that correct?"

"Yes."

"So, is it safe to say you don't believe in discrimination?"

"Of course."

"May I ask, why?"

"Because discrimination is wrong," declared Thomas.

"Ah, "said Josh in an exaggerated way. "So I'm wondering, do you believe that there are certain things that are always wrong?"

"I'm not sure what you mean by that."

"Are there things that are wrong in and of themselves?" Josh challenged.

"In a manner of speaking," Thomas remarked, "but I think that it is more of a case by case basis."

"Okay," Josh humored him. "But wouldn't you consider the act of murder, something that is always wrong?"

"Not if it is in self-defense." Thomas stipulated, as if he had snared him in his trap.

"Good point," Josh acknowledged. "Aside from self-preservation, would you generally say that murder is wrong?"

"Yes," Thomas conceded.

"How about rape?"

"Of course," Thomas answered.

"Is stealing another thing that you would consider wrong?"

"As a rule, yes."

"How about lying?" Josh added for good measure.

"I think sometimes it is necessary." Thomas theorized.

"Like to help you win a court case?" Josh gave a quick little gotcha smile and winked to Clare and to the jury.

"Now you are putting words into my mouth," Thomas said defensively. "I do believe that in certain instances, sometimes telling a small white lie can be helpful."

"Oh, sort of like if my wife was to ask me, if the dress she is wearing - makes her look fat?"

"Exactly," said Thomas, as he was grateful for the explanation.

Josh decided to let Thomas off the hook for now. "But as a general rule, you do believe that lying is wrong."

"Yes," he happily said, thankful that the jury would no longer see him as a liar.

"So to reiterate," Josh reminded him, "you do believe that there are certain behaviors that are inherently wrong such as murder, rape, stealing and even lying."

"That's correct."

"Are you and your partner planning on having a family?"

"We are hoping to adopt at some point."

"That's wonderful." Josh said, trying his best to sound convincing. "And is it safe to say that you would be teaching your child right from wrong?"

"I imagine so." Thomas affirmed, as if he were thinking about it for the very first time.

"So you would be teaching your child that murder is wrong?" Josh asked in earnest.

"I really am hoping," Thomas said grinning to himself, "that's a conversation we actually won't have to sit down and have."

"You've got me there," Josh said smiling. "But if you caught your child stealing, would you let him or her know that it was wrong?"

"Of course," Thomas said with conviction.

"Good. Just to be clear for the jury, you wouldn't actively teach your child that it was okay to lie or steal as long as you don't get caught."

"Absolutely not," Thomas reassured the jury.

"Can you ever see yourself in a situation where you would be coaching any of your children on the best ways to pickpocket strangers or how to burglarize homes?"

"No, I cannot."

"Thank you for your honesty." Josh said sincerely. "Your honor, I was wondering if we could move for an early lunch, I would like some additional time to confer with my clients."

"Since it's almost noon," Justice Hayden declared. "I don't see a problem with that. Ladies and gentlemen of the jury, once again I would like to remind you not to discuss the case with each other or with anyone else for that matter, and please refrain from using any social media. Let's reconvene here at say, 1:15."

a new direction

Josh decided to take them back to the same restaurant. Although they were not able to get a table seated directly in front of the window, they were still situated close enough to be able to observe what was going on in the adjacent park.

Josh broke the silence. "Take a look at the crowd outside – do you think they are right?"

The crowd of protesters had swelled to several hundred, many of which were carrying rainbow flags and some had signs with such slogans as... "Hate Will Never Win"

"Although I can appreciate the message they are trying to convey," Clare said, "somehow I can't shake the feeling that that those signs are directed at us. We don't hate gay people we are called to hate the sin, not the sinner."

"You think they understand that?" Josh challenged emphatically. "To them your beliefs are just as offensive as terrorists who preach radical Islam."

"How could you say such a thing?" Adam demanded.

"How could you be naïve enough to expect them to know the difference? Let me ask you," Josh thought about it for a moment and added. "What do we accomplish if we win this case?"

"We won't go broke for starters," Adam joked, trying his best to lighten the mood.

"That's extremely important," Josh acknowledged. "However, in the grand scheme of things if we prevail, what would we really achieve?"

Clare offered. "Well I guess we would be showing the world that it is important to stand up for religious freedom."

"That's good," said Josh "but wouldn't the same thing be true if you and Adam were Hindus and you owned a catering company and you found yourself on trial because you refused to prepare a steak dinner?"

Clare thought about the scenario for a moment.

"Ever since you came into my office, I've been asking myself why? Was it really simply an accident that our paths crossed or was it some sort of divine intervention? Maybe somebody needs to be the voice of reason. We are rapidly reaching a boiling point to where people aren't even being civil to one another. I'm not sure if you have noticed what's going on outside, and I'm not just talking about right here in this city, but the world is a mess and it's spinning out of control. Everything is being turned on its head. Black is white, up is down and right is wrong. It is becoming harder and harder to know what is true or not."

"Think about it," Josh added. "We live in a country where you can be imprisoned for destroying the egg of a bald eagle, because every sane, rational human being knows that if a bald eagle lays an egg; it will eventually hatch and grow up to be a bald eagle. Yet these very same people have no problem killing an unborn child because in our society, they prefer to think about an unborn child as nothing more than mutated cells. Truth and reason have been turned upside down."

Adam and Clare did their best to soak up what he was saying.

"We have a captive audience, what if instead of arguing the legalities of whether or not you have the right to refuse to do something that goes against your beliefs..."

Josh let the thought evaporate, as he decided to momentarily change directions. "Do you think most people are inherently good or evil?"

"I suspect that most people would like to believe that they are basically good." Clare was quick to reply.

"Why do you think that we are losing?"

"I'm not sure I am following you." Adam piped in.

"Well, if we have the truth on our side, why is Christianity on the decline in this country instead of growing?"

"I can't say for certain," Clare replied, as she wondered about it to herself.

"Perhaps God is using you to help Him tell His story." Josh offered.

"I highly doubt that God needs my help," Clare concluded.

"Despite the fact that no one is perfect, I imagine that most of the population try to live their lives being good. In fact, I'm one hundred percent certain that there are many atheists and agnostics who are genuinely, wonderful people. They do their best not to lie, to steal or otherwise hurt those around them. I'd like to believe that a majority of these people, if they actually knew the truth, would want to follow it."

"I suppose so," Clare acknowledged, even though she wasn't fully convinced herself.

"This entire trial," Josh hinted, "is based upon the fact that you believe God's law supersedes man's law."

"And it does," Adam said as if he were confirming a deep secret.

"I'm not arguing that. I guess what I am trying to say is if God asked you to give up everything you had, to help someone understand the truth ... would it be worth it?"

"What do you mean by worth it?" Clare asked.

"More importantly," Adam interjected, "what do you mean when you say everything?"

"What if, after all is said and done, the court still ruled that you violated the plaintiff's constitutional rights?"

"You are really asking a lot from us," Adam proclaimed, hoping not to sound too selfish.

"Believe me, I know," Josh acknowledged. "Standing up for religious freedom is important, but I think you are in the position to do so much more. Let's play make-believe for a moment. You know those bulletin boards they have outside of most churches?"

"Of course," Clare affirmed.

Josh rummaged around and took a felt tip pen out of his inner suit coat pocket and then proceeded to draw three identical square boxes on the paper napkin that he had placed in front of him.

"Well, if God could choose only one message to convey to the entire world, what do you suppose it would be? Do you really think God would want to have every single church on earth to simultaneously post the phrase..."

And in the first box, Josh neatly wrote as tiny as possible, in all capital letters – MARRIAGE IS MEANT TO BE BETWEEN A MAN AND A WOMAN.

"Perhaps," Josh suggested, "you might be tempted to argue that the sign should read..."

And in the center box he scribbled the phrase YOU MUST REPENT / GOD HATES SIN.

"However, I happen to believe with every fiber of my being that if God could give only one message to the world, it would be..."

In the final box Josh printed GOD LOVES YOU.

"Instead of spending all of our energy defending the traditional definition of marriage, what if we were to use this platform to help others understand the truth?"

"And how would you suggest we do that?"

"What if we were to change tactics?" Josh suggested. "What if we challenged the plaintiffs to defend their beliefs?"

"They don't have any," Clare pointed out. "Or at least since they claim to be atheists, they certainly don't believe in God."

"What if we put them in a position where they were compelled to confront the truth?" Josh hypothesized.

"How could we do that?" Adam wondered aloud.

"I am going to have to think about it for a while, but there has to be a way."

Clare peppered him with questions. "Do you really think that's a wise idea? What makes you so certain that you can accomplish this?"

"I'm not sure. I've been trying to wrap my head around this since the first day you walked into my office. There are literally hundreds if not thousands of attorneys who would have loved to have taken this case. I can't shake the feeling that maybe this was supposed to happen. Maybe everything in our lives," Josh tapped the table rapidly in succession, "has been leading up to this very moment. Right here, right now."

"I think," Josh continued, "that deep down inside every single person on this planet at one time or another has asked themselves "Why am I here?" or "There has to be more to life...""

"But if you are serious about challenging the plaintiffs on their beliefs don't you run the risk of coming across, as you would say ... preachy?" Adam countered.

"Absolutely," said Josh. "There is really no other way around it. Once you bring God into the conversation you automatically run the risk of alienating others. Right now, we have a semi-captive audience. Yes, we run the risk that some people observing this trial will immediately head for the exit never to return, but since they've already invested so much time, perhaps their curiosity might get the better of them and they might choose to stick around just to see how things turn out."

From the looks that Clare and Adam were giving each other, Josh could sense that they were not yet fully convinced.

"What if we could use this court case," Josh explained, "to actually help change people's minds? I happen to think that most people actually want to be good but when it comes to religion, and more specifically God, they have lots of reservations."

"But what good will it do us if we spend all of our time arguing the existence of God," Clare speculated, "if we don't even mention Jesus? How will anyone understand that it is our sins that eternally separate us from God?"

"Again," said Josh, "I am not disagreeing with you but I think we should stick to an argument that we can win. Why would you want to risk offending anyone on the jury?"

"How could telling someone the truth be offensive?" Adam contemplated.

"I think it would be extremely risky to start off by saying that the choices they make will affect how they spend eternity," Josh said emphatically. "Getting someone to think about the afterlife is a bit tricky, and it is quite possible that some people may not even like the idea."

"Why's that?" Clare asked with bona fide interest.

"Sadly, I think some people tend to get bored with this life. I don't think they realize what it would be like to spend eternity with God. To say it would be awesome, would be an understatement of epic proportions. As any parent of a two-year-old will attest, the world is an amazing place when viewed through their eyes. I happen to think spending eternity with God would be a lot like having that same sense of awe and wonder as a toddler only with absolutely no pain or sadness mixed in."

"I'm not quite certain if that is completely biblical, but I think that is a great way of looking at it," Clare confessed.

"But," Josh added, "The reality is that everything about this life screams the here and now. In today's fast paced world, there are holidays, birthdays, bills to pay, deadlines before you know it, another year has gone whizzing by. Getting anyone to focus on eternity may be a difficult task."

"Then what do you suggest?" Clare challenged.

"I think we would be much better off by starting slowly. If we can present a compelling argument for the existence of an All Loving God, maybe they will want to take the time to learn about Him for themselves."

"But how will they know which is the correct path?" Adam cautioned, trying to steer the conversation back to Christianity.

"Although we may both understand that there are a myriad of dead end paths which people can end up going down, I think if we can plant enough seeds, maybe we will be able to point them in the right direction. You have to remember, there are no guarantees with this. People are given the freedom to either accept or reject the truth. Think about it this way...You guys have children, right?" Josh asked, hoping to confirm what he already knew.

"An eight-year-old boy and our daughter is eleven," Clare acknowledged as she smiled at the thought of them.

"Great ages," Josh affirmed. "I want you to think about when they were still infants. I'm sure you can remember that they had to learn to crawl before they could walk?"

"Sure," said Adam.

"As much as you want to explain Christianity, you have to understand that if we are going to succeed here, we need to start with the assumption that at least some of the people we are presenting this evidence to, do not believe that there is a God. I think the best course of action is to first make a really good argument for the existence of God. If, and this is a really big if, we can succeed at this task: then we can see about tackling the next step. Okay?"

"Okay" Clare repeated as she looked over at Adam, still unsure about what they were getting themselves into.

overcome evil with good

"I trust you had a good lunch," Josh asked Thomas in his most sincere voice.

"Actually, we had a great lunch at McCormick's." Thomas divulged.

"Ahhh..." Josh said, giving the restaurant a shameless little plug. "They have the best salmon." He momentarily caught himself reminiscing about how wonderful their food is.

"Sorry, I didn't mean to get side-tracked." Josh continued with his task. "Okay, I believe that just before we broke for lunch you acknowledged that there were certain things that were right and wrong, such as murder, stealing lying..."

"That's correct," Thomas said helpfully.

"Let me ask you; is there such a thing as good and evil?"

After he thought about it, "I'm not so sure." was the only response Thomas could come up with.

"I appreciate your honesty. Well, you've already acknowledged that murder is wrong. Would you consider it evil?"

"I guess it would have to depend on the circumstances," Thomas confided.

"Wow, I have to admit that you really are making some excellent points here today."

"Thank you," said Thomas, as he was momentarily caught off guard by the compliment.

"I'm not talking about," Josh clarified, "a husband that snaps and goes in a fit of rage after he stumbles upon his wife in the midst of an adulterous affair."

Josh paused for a second and looked over at the jury.

"Let's say we are talking about a serial killer that slowly tortures his victims until they die in horrific agony." Josh said, hoping to invoke a response.

"I suppose you could call that evil." Thomas was quick to concede.

"I'm inclined to agree," said Josh. "Do you think Hitler's actions were evil?"

"I try not to think about Hitler."

"Well for the sake of this trial, I would like you to think about him for a moment. Do you think that rounding up six million Jews and sending them to die an agonizing death in the gas chambers was evil? Or was it simply a bit naughty?"

"No, I would have to say it was evil."

"I'd say we are definitely in agreement on that one as well," Josh confirmed.

"Just for the record, would hijacking a plane and flying it into the World Trade Center killing thousands of innocent people be considered evil?"

"I suppose so."

"And if god had instructed his followers to do such a thing?"

"I suppose that if there was a god who inspired his followers to commit such a horrific act, he would have to be evil as well." Thomas divulged, trying his best to humor him.

"Once again, thank you for your honesty. And how about good? Does good exist?"

"I guess it depends," Thomas said. "Does the person doing the good, have ulterior motives?"

"That's another great point. Like if I were to give my wife an expensive gift hoping that I might get a little something, something in return..." Josh gave a mischievous smile and raised his eyebrows up and down a few times in quick succession. Enough to elicit a few giggles from some of the women on the jury.

"Like I said," Thomas reiterated, "ulterior motives."

"What about someone who donates a kidney to a complete stranger so that they might live, would that qualify as good?"

Thomas thought about it for a moment, "Yes, I think that would qualify as good."

"How about someone who rushes in to a burning building to save the people trapped inside."

"I'd call that good too."

"So, although it is possible that we may differ on what we consider to be both good and evil, we are in agreement that they do exist."

"Yes," Thomas confirmed.

"It really is amazing," Josh mused, "as to how many different things we can agree upon."

Thomas smiled at the thought.

"Now I understand that you don't believe in God, but I would like to play make believe for a moment."

"Objection – Relevance? Jeremy interjected hoping to stop this line of questioning.

"If it pleases the court, my clients are on trial because of their belief in God. I think it is important for the jury to understand what, if any, thoughts the plaintiff may or may not have regarding the topic of God."

"I'm going to allow it," Justice Hayden affirmed.

"You are aware that my clients believe in God."

"Yes."

"And," Josh continued "they believe that not only is God All-Knowing and All Powerful but All Loving as well."

"I've heard God described in those terms before," Thomas conferred, doing his best to humor Josh.

"I know this is just a theological exercise, but if there really was a God capable of creating the universe in a split second," Josh snapped his fingers to emphasize the point. "If such a God did exist, would it be a good idea to be on His good side?"

"If such a God existed, I suppose so," Thomas agreed.

"And if this God did exist would He have a right to make up some rules?"

"If there really was a God, then I guess he could make up whatever rules he wanted." Thomas said with a heavy sigh as though he were exasperated with this silly game.

"Fantastic, I appreciate you humoring me with this exercise. Oh," as if he had almost forgotten, "If there really was a God, do you think He would have the right to judge us?"

"Objection – Speculation" Jeremy responded.

"Your honor," Josh continued "we have already established that the witness does not believe in God and that he is merely responding to a hypothetical argument."

"I will allow it; you may answer the question."

"I guess if there was a God, I suppose he could judge us if he wanted."

"Thank you for playing along with me," said Josh. "There is one more thing I almost forgot. If there really was a God, and we were all his children, could you ever imagine a loving parent telling some of His children to kill their siblings?"

"That would be ridiculous." Thomas said, with shocking honesty.

"If I am understanding you correctly, you couldn't imagine a loving God that hated Canadians?"

"Why on earth would God hate Canadians?"

"He wouldn't," Josh agreed, "it's just a hypothetical question. But just to clarify things, if there was a God that hated Canadians, for whatever reason - do you agree that it would be impossible for Him to be considered an all loving God?"

"If there really was such a thing as an all loving God, he would, by definition, have to love everyone – even Canadians."

"Thank you for your insight," Josh replied.

Justice Hayden looked over and saw that it was pushing four o'clock. "I think this might be a good time for us to wrap things up for today. Mr. Addicott, you are free to step down but I want to remind you that when this court reconvenes tomorrow, you are going to be back up here on the witness stand."

"Yes, your honor." Thomas said in his most respectful voice.

"Ladies and Gentlemen of the jury," Justice Hayden announced. "I'm sure you know the drill by now but I still need to remind you not to discuss the case with anyone and once again, please avoid all forms of news and social media. Thank you so very much for your time and we will see you here tomorrow at nine."

After the judge had left the courtroom, Clare leaned towards Josh and asked, "How do you think we are doing?"

"There is really no way to tell so far. I'm happy we were allowed to at least get the hypothetical questions about God into official record."

"Why is that?" Clare wondered curiously.

"Well if we are to have any chance of swaying either the plaintiff or anyone on the jury, it is critical that they understand that if God does exist, He is all powerful, all knowing and all loving."

"Why would that be so important?" Clare said hoping to understand the process a little bit better.

"If we fail to establish all His attributes at the beginning it might be harder for the members of the jury to understand that God knows everything about them right down to the very last detail. If they are going to go back and deliberate about it, I want them to understand that God knows all the disgusting things they have ever done or thought in their entire life."

"Also," Josh explained, "that by establishing that God is all loving it helps on two folds. It would automatically rule out a god that doesn't love: but more importantly, it will help jurors to understand that God will forgive them no matter what they have done."

"I think I'm beginning to understand," said Clare thoughtfully.

"We still have a very long way to go and this is definitely going to be an uphill battle. Keep in mind, up until this point we have done absolutely zero to convince anyone that there even is a God. Everything that we've done so far, has been purely hypothetical."

Itching to get his chance to help out, Adam once again volunteered, "I still would like you to put me on the stand."

Clare added "We would also like you to introduce the fact that there can only be one path to take. Proving the existence of God without talking about Jesus, won't do a lot of good."

"Let's concentrate on one step at a time," Josh emphasized. "If we cannot convince anyone that there is a God, what makes you think that telling them about His Son would make any sense? I know I am probably repeating myself but this is a step by step process and we are still a long way from the finish line. I want you to go home relax and let me try and figure out what needs to be done next."

all things are possible

When Josh got back to his car, he let out a heavy sigh. What the hell have I gotten myself into he thought to himself? Happy for any distraction, he decided to talk to his wife.

"Siri, dial Susan."

The phone rang and Susan answered in her usual cheery greeting. From the way Josh responded, she knew immediately that something was wrong.

Josh proceeded to tell her the story. "...the next thing I know I am suggesting that instead of trying to win the trial, we should be trying to prove the existence of God."

"What? Do you understand how insane that sounds?"

"I can't explain how or why it happened, it just sort of came out of me. The strangest part is that it really didn't take that much convincing to get the Robinsons on board."

"Can you go back to the original plan?"

"It's possible; as of right now, besides my clients, you are the only other person that knows what we are trying to do."

"And how much is on the line?"

"If we lose, we are talking about three hundred and fifty thousand dollars."

"Hon, you can't let them lose that kind of money."

"I really wish I had a good explanation," Josh said shaking his head to himself. "It doesn't even make sense to me. The only thing I can say for certain is that this feels like something I am supposed to be doing."

Susan said "I hope to God you are right."

Josh let out a heavy sigh. "Do you trust me?"

"You know I do," Susan said with conviction.

"And do you love me?"

"You know I do." Susan repeated.

"Then I am going to ask for your help, because I can't do this without you in my corner."

"I really hope you know what you are getting yourself into." Susan said, as she shook her head into the phone.

"So do I," Josh revealed, and barely whispered it a second time. "So do I."

"Anyway, it's probably a good thing you are at your mom's right now because I've got lots of work to do and I suspect it is going to be a very late night for me. I'm definitely going to have to get some help on this one," Josh added.

"Are you going to talk to Matt?"

"He's the logical choice."

"Give him my best. Love you."

Josh ended the conversation with his usual "Love you more."

I am the light, the truth, the way

The big burly biker nearly crushed him with his bear hug. "Good to see you councilor."

"Right back at ya my friend. How are things with you?"

"All is, as it should be," said Matt cryptically. Two months shy of his sixtieth birthday Matt Sullivan was not only imposing, but intimidating as well. He still carried his hulking frame as if the next barroom brawl was right around the corner. It had been a long time since he had worn colors, but his tattooed arms still verified his checkered past.

"Glad to hear it," said Josh. "As you may have heard, I have decided to take on the first amendment case."

"The bakers?" Matt said in an inquisitive tone.

"That's the one."

"Well good for you," Matt said grinning. "It's about time you had a respectable client."

Josh looked at him and smiled because he knew how and why they first met.

"You know me," said Josh "I'm a big proponent of second chances. I've got a little dilemma, and I was wondering if I could get your help?"

"My help?" Matt acted as if this was the most puzzling thing he had ever heard.

"Well, we've decided to change tactics and we are now going to argue the existence of God."

"In court?" Matt said, with exaggerated disbelief.

"I know, I know," Josh repeated, "but I was thinking that since we have a semi-captive audience, it might be possible to sway a juror or two."

"Whoa," said Matt, "Don't you think you are severely underestimating the stupidity of your fellow human beings. Think about it. People will happily believe in ghosts, U.F.O.s, the Loch Ness Monster even Bigfoot but try introducing something as controversial as God and people will think you are delusional at best."

"Yup."

Matt expelled an exaggeratedly long high-pitched whistle, like a bomb being dropped from a plane. "You've got a brass set my friend. And all this time

I actually thought you were pretty intelligent." The warmth in his smile betrayed his attempt at sarcasm.

"That's not the worst part," Josh confessed. "They don't just want me to prove the existence of God: my clients are pretty adamant that I should bring Jesus into the equation."

"Is that all?" teased Matt. "I don't envy you my friend."

"Thanks, I really appreciate that. I was just hoping for a little input."

"And what does this have to do with me?"

"You've been around the block a few times..."

"That's it, ask for my help and throw me under the bus at the same time." Matt said, as he did his best to try and look like he was hurt.

"Well, without using the scriptures, I need to find a way to prove that Jesus is who He claimed to be."

"Wowzers," Matt said in astonishment. He couldn't comprehend how his friend could get himself boxed into a corner like that.

"Yup, I was hoping you might be able to provide an angle I hadn't thought about."

"Are you insane? Does Susan know about this?"

"Only the first part, she is worried enough as it is and I didn't think there was any need to make her more nervous. She sends her love by the way."

Just thinking about Susan brought a smile to Matt's face. "And this was their idea?"

"You're going to think I'm an even bigger idiot. The trial was actually going along quite well. This is the type of case most lawyers dream about. We have the law on our side and even if we lose this round, this is probably one of those cases which could go all the way to the Supreme Court"

"So why the change?"

"I really can't explain why, it just sort of tumbled out of me. The next thing I know I am convincing my clients that we would be better served going in a new direction."

"I'm glad I'm not in your shoes." Matt said shaking his head.

"Thanks."

"Oh," Matt said sarcastically, "don't mention it."

"Here's my predicament, I think I can come up with a pretty good argument for God, but I am stumped as to how I can introduce Jesus into the courtroom."

"Can you go back to the original plan?"

"That's exactly what Susan said," Josh proclaimed, as he laughed to himself.

"I knew there was a reason why I love her," Matt divulged.

"Anyway, that's why I am here. I was hoping to pick your brain."

"I'm afraid that there's not much left."

"Trust me, I'm well aware," Josh said laughing.

"Like I told you, my clients are pretty adamant about wanting me to talk about Jesus. My dilemma stems from the fact that I can't walk up to the jury and hand them all a copy of the bible and say, read this and it will help you understand exactly why Jesus is who He claims to be."

"Why not?" Matt said, looking confused.

"Couple of reasons," said Josh. "The first is that the odds are there will probably be a few atheists on the jury. Not to mention that there could be people of other faiths so convincing anyone that the Bible is God's Word might be out of the question. The second problem is time. I really don't know how long this trial will last but I am certain that I won't have an unlimited amount of time in which to convince the jury."

"Wow, you must really enjoy a challenge." Matt surmised.

"But can you help?"

"Let me get this straight, you want me to help prove that Jesus is the Son of God but we can't use the Bible to do so."

"Yup!" Josh said with a straight face. "Can't even cross reference it."

"Is it safe to assume that everyone on the jury will know who Jesus is?" Matt asked, as he shook his head thinking about the predicament his friend was in.

"I think that the only thing we can say for sure is that the odds are pretty good that everyone has at least heard His name."

"Do you think they would know His story?"

"What do you mean by His story?"

"Do you think they would know that He died on the cross?"

"I'm not sure," Josh mused, "but even if they knew that part, they probably wouldn't know why He died."

"What other details do you think they might know?"

"That's a tricky one. I could throw out some pretty well-known verses such as "Love Thy Neighbor" and "Do Unto Others," but there are no guarantees that everyone would be familiar with even these."

"Talk about being between a rock and a hard place." Matt didn't envy his friend's predicament.

"I didn't come here so you could remind me of what a pickle I'm in," Josh teased him.

Matt gave a heavy sigh. "This is a tough one on such short notice."

"I was really hoping you might be up to the task."

"It's just a head scratcher that's all." Matt rested his chin atop of his meaty folded paws. "This might not come out right because I am trying to do this in real time, so please bear with me."

Matt thought about it for a few seconds... "Okay try this one on for size. If someone actually came here and claimed that He was the Son of God, logically I can only think of three possible explanations that would make sense."

"The first option would be that he is a lunatic. He is completely out of his mind – perhaps due to drugs, alcohol or some sort of mental defect. The second would be that he is lying; he knows that there is no such thing as God but he thinks that by saying he is God's Son he will gain something. Maybe he wants money, power or even fame. The third possibility would be that there really is a God and He is telling the truth."

"So how does that help us?" Josh asked hoping for a more detailed explanation.

"If you break it down, step by step: First let's look at the possibility that He is a lunatic? If you examine Jesus' life in detail, everything screams NO. If you listen to what He was teaching it makes absolute sense. He understood that we are all brothers and sisters; we are all in this world together so we should have compassion and love one another. He taught us that we need to have patience and we need to forgive one another. He understood that because nobody is perfect and we have all made mistakes, we should not judge one another. Everything He taught was one hundred percent true."

"That makes sense," Josh agreed.

"Let's look at the second possibility. He was lying. It is possible but... people lie for a reason. Either it is for money or power or some sort of personal gain. Jesus gained nothing while He was here. He didn't become rich; he didn't become powerful and he actually went to His death because of what He was teaching. If Jesus knew that He was making the whole story up, that there really wasn't a God, why would He willingly go to His death? He had absolutely nothing to gain by lying."

"That brings us to the third possibility," said Matt. "Jesus is, in fact, who He claims to be. I'm not trying to confuse you, but here is something else to ponder. Imagine if Jesus knew there was a God and He was only pretending to be His Son. Don't you think that would make Him a liar of biblical proportions?"

"I'd have to agree with that one." Josh acknowledged.

"Think about this for comparison," Matt said continuing his thought process. "Hitler never claimed to be a nice guy. He was responsible for killing over 6 million Jews. Over the last two thousand years, how many Christians went to their graves putting their trust in Jesus?

"I'm guessing that number would have to be at least in the hundreds of millions, if not billions," Josh concluded.

"So, if Jesus was lying," Matt proclaimed, "I would have to say that it makes Him far worse than Hitler."

"I never thought about it that way but it really puts things into perspective. I think that it is a really great argument but I still can't use it in court," Josh confided.

"Why not?" asked Matt.

"Because even though everything you are saying is true, you are assuming too much. As I said before, I have to expect that the jury will be a pretty good sampling of our population at large. There could be Muslims, Hindus, Buddhist and even atheists on that jury. Who knows, there might be a Scientologist or even a Pagan?"

"What difference would that make?" Matt said trying to find out where he was going with this.

"I can't expect that everyone on that jury will have a complete understanding of who Jesus was or what He was teaching. I can't insist that they go home and learn about Him for themselves. If this is going to work, I need to stick with an argument that will make sense."

"Okay, I see what you are getting at. If I'm understanding you correctly, this may have to be a one-shot deal."

"Exactly."

"Have you thought about mentioning His Disciples?"

"What about 'em?"

"Well, they hung out with Him on a daily basis for almost three years."

"And your point would be?"

"Well, they watched Him do all these amazing miracles and still they weren't one hundred percent certain if He was who He claimed to be."

"I don't see how that helps us."

"You didn't even give me a chance to finish." Matt complained.

"Well, couldn't someone argue that Jesus was simply extremely intelligent, charismatic and He had some great ideas that were ahead of His time?" Josh said defiantly.

"Of course," Matt continued, "but that wouldn't explain what happened after He died on the cross. Think about it, when He was alive, in addition to the thousands of people who flocked to see Him, He had a group of twelve disciples that He taught on a daily basis. They understood that there was something different about Him. It wasn't that He was simply more intelligent than those around Him or that He could do some neat magic tricks, they understood that He was not like everyone else. I think that what really upset the leaders at the time was that He had the audacity to claim that God was His Father. Well, here they are after following Him around for three years, and they watched Him die on the cross. Try to envision it. This was one of their closest friends. They watched Him get publicly executed. They actually went to His funeral. One would think after all that, it would have been the end of the movement."

"It's a good argument but I don't think I can use it," Josh said, interrupting him again.

"Don't you see," Matt emphasized, "if Jesus simply died on the cross, His following would have ended right there. But that's not the end of the story. It's just the beginning. When His followers saw Him alive again it was pretty hard to ignore. After His resurrection, it added so much more credibility to His claim that God was His Father. Sadly, most of His disciples also died in agony. You would expect that if they were not one hundred percent certain that they saw Jesus alive again, as they were being tortured, they would eventually break down and admit that they made everything up. But that's not what happened. They all went to their deaths fully convinced that they were on the right path. Not only that, but the movement continued to grow. You need to ask yourself ... why would anyone willingly go to their death to defend something that they knew to be a lie? Or why would anyone willingly join a group that resulted in death, if they knew it was merely a hoax?"

"I still can't use it," Josh reemphasized. "It is circumstantial evidence at best. There are definitely no eyewitnesses that can be brought into court. If I were that plaintiff's attorney, I would simply argue Here-Say. I'm sure that a lot of people today would rationalize that there is no way to know for certain what happened two thousand years ago. I just think it might be hard to prove in court."

"It all goes back to the fact that people lie for a reason," Matt emphasized. "If His followers were not 100% certain that they saw Jesus alive again, why would they willingly go to their death pretending they did? What could they possibly hope to gain by lying?"

"I like the argument and it would definitely give the jury something to think about. Perhaps I can see if there is a way I can introduce it into the case," Josh speculated.

"If you decline to use these arguments as proof that Jesus is who He claims to be, then I hate to tell you this, but I'm thinking you might want to consider reversing directions."

"I was really hoping for better advice than that my friend."

"I'm sorry, you're right." Matt thought about it for a moment. "This one might be a little bit of a stretch, but you said you feel pretty confident that you can come up with a good argument for the existence of God?"

"Confident might be a bit of an exaggeration," Josh corrected him.

Matt looked at his friend as if he were smoking crack. "Still," ignoring his last comments, "if you can convince the jury that there is a God, maybe you can convince the jury that Jesus has to be?"

"I don't get it, I'm not sure I'm following you on this one."

"Well when you were in court, did you get to describe the attributes of God?"

"We touched upon it."

"So the jury would understand that God was all knowing, all loving and all powerful?"

"They were informed, whether or not it will sink in is anyone's guess?"

"Did you get a chance to tell them that God was Holy?

"No, I didn't go down that road." Josh said. "I wasn't sure that they would understand."

"Well, you did talk about good and evil, right and wrong?"

"Yeah, we covered that."

"Well, the next step shouldn't be too hard."

"What do you mean?"

"You would need to get the jury to understand that God is perfect: perfect in every sense of the word. There is no deceit, no dishonesty, and no corruption. He is so perfect that He can't even be in the presence of sin. Then you could inform them that His Son willingly went to His death to accept the punishment for our sins?"

"I'm not sure if I can use the word sins in the courtroom."

"Fine, choose another word, our crimes, our transgressions, our immorality.... Whatever? I think that if people are really being honest with themselves they will admit that even though they may try to be good and decent people, they know that there are times when they have fallen short. People lie, people steal, and people cheat, we manipulate one another. It's what we do."

"But that still doesn't explain why He had to die?" Josh said hoping for a better explanation.

"Here's a good example," said Matt. "I want you to think about an operating room. Something so sterile that even the tiniest speck of dirt could contaminate it. The only way to enter such a room is to become sterile yourself."

"Okay."

Matt continued. "Now think about God as this perfect being. So perfect in fact, that He cannot come into contact with anyone who isn't perfect themselves."

Josh thought about the image his friend was painting.

"But," Matt continued, "What if God loved us so much that He had the perfect plan to help us spend eternity with Him? What if His Son willingly went to His death to pay the price for our sins? Think of Jesus' death as a cleansing action. He shed His blood to wash us clean of all our imperfections."

"I'm still not sure if that would be something I could use in court."

"Can't you see? If you could explain to the jury that there really is a perfect and Holy God, and we need to be perfect ourselves in order to be in His presence, then His Son offering up His life as a sacrifice for our sins, would make perfect sense."

Matt patiently waited for a response and when none came, he continued. "Since we can never be perfect because every single one of us has, at one time or another; lied, cheated, stolen ... we are all guilty. This is where Jesus comes into play. He agreed to take on our punishment for us. This is a free gift but we have to decide whether or not we want to accept it."

"You know I love you brother. I'm not saying that it isn't a good argument and I actually think it might help someone to understand who Jesus was, and why He had to die but I'm still at the same place I was before, there really isn't any way I can bring that up in court."

"Look, you're an attorney."

"Thanks for noticing," Josh sarcastically replied.

"I try," Matt teased. "Think of Jesus as the ultimate attorney."

"And how will that help?"

"Keep on thinking about it my friend; I'm sure it will come to you."

"This is turning out to be a lot harder than I thought it would," Josh confided.

"Are you really sure you want to do this?"

"Trust me: I am definitely questioning my sanity on this one." Josh confessed.

"Just this one?" Matt said in a joking manner.

"You've got me there. Anyway, thanks for your help but I think I might need a more worldly point of view."

"Seriously?"

"Yup."

"Are you guys coming on Sunday?"

"Susan's still at her mom's and won't be home until later that afternoon, but I'll be there."

"Fantastic, see you then. One more thing," Matt divulged, "try not to stress. I know you probably don't want to hear this, but I believe sometimes people do their best work when their backs are up against the wall. You'd be amazed at what you can accomplish if you put your mind to it."

"Thanks for the vote of confidence."

let no one deceive himself

Everyone took their respective places back in the courtroom; the jurors were ushered back into the jury box, Thomas was escorted back to the witness stand.

Justice Hayden said "I want to remind you that you are still under oath."

Thomas nodded and said, "I understand."

"Good Morning Mr. Addicott welcome back. How are you doing today?"

"Fantastic."

"If you don't mind," Josh said, "I'd like to go back to a statement you made the other day. I asked you if you believed in evolution and your reply was, and I quote, all the evidence seems to indicate so."

"Objection – Asked and Answered," said Jeremy defiantly.

"If it pleases the court," Josh interjected, "I know we have already touched upon this topic briefly but at this time I feel it is necessary to get a little bit more clarification on the plaintiff's beliefs."

"I'm going to allow it," Justice Hayden said. "Overruled."

"So," Josh continued, "in your previous testimony we were talking about evolution and you replied that all the evidence seems to indicate that it is a proven fact. Is that correct?"

"Yes it is."

"And just to refresh the jury, scientists claim that the earth is approximately four point five billion years old- is that correct?"

"Yes, I believe that those are the generally accepted numbers."

"And at one point the earth was nothing more than a chunk of molten rock."

"Objection – Speculation. "As my client was not an eye witness to these events, he should not be called to testify as to what did or did not happen some four and a half billion years ago." Jeremy argued, hoping to slow down this line of questioning.

"Once again your honor," Josh protested, "I am not asking for an eye witness testimony, but I would like to request a little leeway as it goes to establish the plaintiff's beliefs."

"I'm going to allow it. You may answer the question." Justice Hayden decided.

"That's what scientists claim." Thomas said, in a most convincing manner.

"And you subscribe to these beliefs?"

"Yes I do."

"Thank you. So getting back to the formulation of the earth, at one time there was absolutely no life on this planet, is that correct?"

"Objection – Asked and answered," Jeremy demanded.

"Yes," Thomas, confirmed anyway.

"But there is certainly life now." Josh mused, as if there was some sort of contradiction.

"Of course." Thomas acknowledged, leaning into the microphone.

"So at one point," Josh paused for effect, "something changed."

"Obviously," Thomas said with a smirk, which caused a few members of the jury to quietly giggle.

"Okay," Josh said holding up his index finger for dramatic effect. "At any point in your life have you ever witnessed, no let me rephrase that, have you ever heard about non-living material spontaneously transforming itself into life?"

"I'm not sure I understand the question?" Thomas asked with all sincerity.

"Let me give you an example," Josh said, trying his best to be helpful. He walked back to his table and picked up a softball-sized, semi pointy rock and held it up for dramatic effect. "Have you ever heard of a rock suddenly transforming itself into some kind of animal?"

"No... I have not," Thomas replied.

"Have you ever heard of a rock turning itself into a plant?"

"No, I have not."

"I'm sorry," said Josh, "could you repeat that for the jury."

"No I have not." Thomas admitted.

"What we have here is a bit of a dilemma. Because we are currently having this conversation, I think most reasonable people will agree that we are both alive."

Thomas nodded his head and in a barely audible voice said, "Sure."

"But at some point," Josh articulated, as he gently tossed the rock up and down in the palm of his hand, "the earth was nothing but rocks. Wait, let me rephrase that, the earth was nothing but molten lava. Yet, we can both agree … something changed. Somehow life appeared. Despite all the scientific advances we've made, experts are still uncertain as to exactly what happened. Do you have any explanations for this jury?"

Jeremy rose slightly from his seat. "Objection – The witness never claimed to be an expert in this field."

"Your honor," Josh protested, "I am merely trying to re-establish the beliefs held by the plaintiff."

"Overruled, I'm going to allow it."

"I've never really given it much thought." Thomas truthfully admitted to the jury.

"One would think that with all the technology available, some scientist somewhere, would have been able to take a bunch of rocks, toss them in some boiling water, maybe add a battery or two for some electricity and prove once and for all that life is capable of spontaneously arising from non-life."

"Speculation - your honor," said Jeremey hoping to take back control of the conversation.

"Sustained," Justice Hayden readily agreed. "Please strike that last comment from the record."

"Is it your belief that at some point in our history, life formed from nothing more than water and rocks and over the course of millions of years we have evolved from a simple, one-celled organism all the way up to the wonderful creatures we see before us today?"

"I'm not so sure everyone would agree that all humans are wonderful." Thomas said, garnering a few laughs.

"But those," Josh recounted, "are your overall beliefs, is that correct?"

"Yes."

"Do you also agree that one of the primary functions of each species is to pass along their genes so that succeeding generations will ensue?"

"Of course," Thomas said without hesitation. "Without reproduction, a species will die off."

"Once again," Josh said politely, "thank you for your candor. Since the concept of God has been around for thousands of years, it stands to reason that at some point in our history, you believe our ancestors felt a need to invent Him?"

"Perhaps," Thomas offered, "they felt that they needed a way to explain things that they could not understand?"

"That makes sense," said Josh. "I suspect that thousands of years ago people did not fully understand how weather works like we do today, so I imagine the concept of thunder and lightning must have been pretty frightening."

"Exactly," Thomas proclaimed, as he felt that Josh was finally beginning to see the light.

"So in order to explain these natural forces," Josh continued, "they decided to attribute them to some sort of God"?

"Yes," said Thomas smiling.

"I have to admit," Josh speculated, "that really does sound plausible."

"Maybe there is hope for you after all." Thomas asserted, as he silently declared victory to himself.

"I am trying my best to avoid any ambiguity here. Are you trying to tell this jury that it is your conclusion that at some point in earth's history, our ancestors felt the need to invent a mystical being and call it God simply because they did not understand certain natural phenomenon such as thunder, lightning and earthquakes?"

"Because I was not there," Thomas said defensively, "I am not sure if that is exactly how it happened, but I suspect it was something like that."

"Now I am starting to follow your sense of logic. Was it always just one particular God?"

"I imagine that in the beginning our ancestors probably had many gods."

"So a god of thunder, a god of lightning maybe a sun god?" Josh hinted.

"Now you are getting it," Thomas readily agreed.

"So over time, as we evolved, these various different gods simply morphed into one God?" Josh theorized.

"Perhaps it may have been more of a control issue," Thomas deduced.

"I think I am following you now. Because the Greeks had their set of gods and the Romans had their set of gods, are you saying it was sort of like my God is more powerful than your god sort of thing?

How wonderfully delicious Thomas thought to himself, now I've got him right where I want him. "What better way of controlling the masses?" he explained.

"Ah" said Josh thoughtfully. "So, I would imagine that you subscribe to the Karl Marx quote about religion being the opiate of the masses?"

"Absolutely." Thomas admitted to the courtroom. "I'm actually quite fond of that quote."

"And what does that quote mean to you?" Josh asked.

"I would say," as Thomas turned his attention toward the jury, "that religion allows discontented people the ability to suppress their discomfort in this life, by placing a belief in a promise of a better afterlife."

"Well said."

"Thank you," Thomas replied gratefully, as he smiled at the jurors.

"It sounds as though you have given this some thought," Josh complimented him.

"Perhaps I read it somewhere, but I try to look at the world as objectively as possible." Thomas boasted.

"Is it correct to assume that you believe that man invented god as a way of explaining things that he could not understand?"

"Yes."

"But at some point," Josh thoughtfully added, "our ancestors decided that not only would this fictitious god have sovereignty over all the natural forces in the world such as wind and rain, but he would also act as some sort of judge: ruling over right and wrong?"

"What better way to control the population?" Thomas affirmed, with satisfied glee.

"Okay, I think I'm following you now. As societies became more complex, it became necessary to have more rules, and what better way to get people to follow these rules, than to say that they come from god?"

"Now you are helping to prove my point about the absurdity of religion."

"One thing that puzzles me," Josh concluded. "Before they decided to attribute these rules to their mystical god that they made up ... did these rules exist?"

"What do you mean?" Thomas asked in earnest.

"What I am trying to say, is that right now we can agree that it is wrong to murder, it is also wrong to steal, that it is wrong to rape. I may be going out on a limb, but I would venture to guess that most people would even agree that it is wrong to lie. What I am asking you here today, is if you believe that these are universal truths which exist outside of time?"

"I'm not sure I'm following you."

"I know you are a very smart man," Josh said in his most sincere voice. "Has it always been wrong to murder or is that something that has evolved along with us? I want to make this crystal clear, go back as far into our history as you like... except for certain conditions such as self-defense or protecting one's family – has it always been wrong to take another person's life?"

Thomas thought about it for a moment and eventually gave in. "I suppose so,"

"I apologize for any miscommunication here, but I'm trying to get a little certainty. If you go far enough back into our history, would it have been wrong for one caveman to bash another caveman in the head with a rock?"

"I would have to say yes."

"I'm sorry," Josh feigned momentary auditory loss, "I didn't quite hear you. Could you please repeat that for the courtroom?"

"I said yes," Thomas repeated.

"Thank you, and what about theft? Could you imagine a time where theft would not have been considered wrong?"

"There was probably a point in our history where no one had any possessions." Thomas challenged.

"Oh, you mean back when we were still living in caves?"

"Yes," Thomas said, as if he were talking to a five-year-old.

"But at some point," Josh added "we would have started to develop tools? If one caveman spent hours and hours sharpening a nice pointy rock so that it became a spearhead, would it have been wrong for another member of the tribe to simply take it?"

"I guess so."

"Now if the caveman who spent hours making the spear confronted the one who took it, and the person who took it; let's call him a thief for lack of a better word, denied taking it: would lying about the theft be wrong as well?"

"Yes."

"Once again to clarify things for the courtroom, you are in agreement that taking another person's life has always been wrong. Taking another person's property is also something that has always been wrong. And denying the truth – or lying is something that has always been wrong."

"It seems like it," Thomas replied, in an almost defeated tone.

"One thing that perplexes me about your beliefs, if these natural laws have always been in existence; where do you suppose that they come from?"

"I never really thought about it."

"That's okay," said Josh. "For now, the important thing is that we are in agreement that these moral truths do exist."

"I don't know if I would go so far as to call them moral truths."

"Okay, what would you call them?"

"I guess you could call them natural or inherent laws," Thomas declared, with an air of rationality.

"Perfect, I like that term – inherent laws. Now when you were sworn in, you took an oath to tell the truth do you remember that?"

"Yes, I remember that," Thomas humored him as he rolled his eyes ever so slightly.

"It seems a bit strange to me... why do you think that in a cold and impersonal universe, the concept of truth even exists?"

"I'm not sure I understand the question."

"Sure, you do, but let me give you an example." Josh reached inside his inner suit coat pocket and pulled out a shiny, gold Cross pen and held it up for the jury to see.

"If I took this pen," Josh walked over to the witness stand and pretended to hand it to Thomas. Instead, at the very last second, he pulled his hand away and in an exaggerated fashion, opened his suit jacket and clearly placed the pen in his shirt pocket.

"Now if I told the jury," Josh added as he held up his finger, "that I handed you the pen, that would be a lie ... because everyone here witnessed that I did not. So, if there is such a thing as a lie, then there must also be such a thing as truth. Hopefully you'll agree that it is impossible for something to be true and untrue at the very same time. My question to you is, why does truth exist?"

"I don't have an answer."

"Have you ever taken the time to think about where truth comes from? I imagine when you are trying to rationalize the exact origins of truth, you will be using some sort of logic. Yet, isn't logic itself, further proof that we do indeed live in a world that is governed by natural laws? Or do you honestly think that it is your own personal, highly-evolved brain that developed the concept of logic and deductive reasoning for the benefit of the entire universe?"

"I've never tried to claim that," Thomas said, defensively.

"One more thing," Josh added as an afterthought. "If a person in this room, let's say your attorney ... were to claim that I handed you the pen when they know that I did not, they would be lying right?"

"That would be correct."

"So, if someone actually knows the truth and then deliberately lied about it, wouldn't most rational people be suspicious of their motives?"

"I certainly would be." Thomas revealed.

"Your honor, with your permission, I think this might be as good a time as any to break for lunch."

Justice Hayden looked up and saw that it was almost noon and happily agreed.

After the usual instructions, the court was adjourned.

a fly in the ointment

Once the waitress had taken all the orders, Adam was the first to jump back into the conversation.

"I thought we were trying to help the jury understand that God exists, not the other way around?"

Josh patiently let Adam vocalize his concerns and once he was done. "Before I get started, is there anything else you need to ask me?"

"No," Adam said, feeling a bit ashamed of his outburst.

"This is probably not what you are going to want to hear, but I think it might be a good idea if we took this case back to its original course."

"What are you talking about? Adam asked not wanting to believe what he was hearing.

"I've got a bit of a dilemma," Josh revealed. "Getting the plaintiff to talk about his beliefs is relatively easy: introducing Jesus is a whole different kettle of fish. Remember I was telling you that it was more than likely that, at most, there would be three or four people on the jury who considered themselves to be Christian?"

"Yes," said Clare.

"Well, it is possible that not everyone on the jury knows who Jesus is."

"So, can't you just explain?" Adam proposed in a concerned voice.

"Yes and no," Josh said, confusing them even more. "It all comes back to what we can prove in court."

Not wanting to abandon the project in midstream, Adam thought about how he could help to keep Josh from throwing in the towel.

"Do you think," Adam surmised "that it is a safe assumption that most members of the jury would accept that some two thousand years ago there was a man named Jesus?"

"I suspect that there could possibly be someone on the jury who might even be skeptical about that," Josh said honestly.

"Maybe you could point out that because there is no one here on this planet today that was living when George Washington was alive," Clare offered, "that there is no definitive way that we can prove that he existed."

Josh shot back, "We can because of history books."

"Exactly," said Clare. "Doesn't it seem a bit implausible to think that there has been so much written about a fictitious character that never even lived? There are way more books written about Jesus Christ than Julius Caesar, yet most people have no trouble accepting that Caesar was real."

"Okay, that's a good point. I can go with the assumption that everyone on the jury will accept that there was a person called Jesus who walked this earth, but this is where things get a bit tricky. I mean, how much does the average person actually know?"

"I think it is safe to say that they might know about Christmas and Easter and that He had some pretty radical ideas such as love thy enemies and turn the other cheek." Adam said constructively.

"We still have time," Clare said, refusing to let this go down in flames. "Let's see how things proceed this afternoon and we can go from there."

Josh let out a heavy sigh, "I guess that's probably the best thing we can do for now."

"So that means you are planning on staying the course?" Adam challenged.

"At least for the time being," said Josh, "yes."

Adam looked over at Clare and she was smiling. "That's good enough for us."

he who has ears, let him hear

After what Josh considered a less than fruitful lunch, everyone returned to the courtroom and he proceeded with his interrogation of Thomas.

"Picking up where we left off, you originally expressed that you believe in evolution," Josh reiterated. "Is that correct?"

"Objection," said Jeremy – "Asked and answered."

"Let me rephrase that," said Josh. "Do you believe that every living being on earth is also evolving as well?"

"That would make sense," Thomas replied, as if he was thinking about it for the very first time.

"So," Josh continued his train of thought, "I would imagine that at some point – maybe millions and millions of years from now, lions would evolve to a point where they no longer killed other animals for food."

"Now you are just being ridiculous," said Thomas.

"Why?" Josh said trying to lead him down the desired path.

"Because lions are carnivores," Thomas unsuspectingly obliged. "They need to kill for survival."

"But over time, wouldn't they evolve to a point where they no longer needed to hunt for food?"

"I'm not sure it works that way?"

"Then how does it work?" Josh said, as if he was completely confused.

"I can't say for certain," Thomas confessed.

"Once again, thank you for your honesty. But if it is a matter of evolution, then it stands to reason that every single creature on this planet is also evolving. Maybe not at the same speed, but wouldn't it make sense that at some point all animals would evolve to where they understood that killing is wrong."

"I guess anything is possible." Thomas decided.

"You can't guess," Josh lectured. "After all, didn't you say that evolution is a proven science?"

"I've never really taken the time to think about it that way."

"That's okay," Josh said, easing up on the accelerator just a bit. "Most people don't."

Josh paused, folded his hands and looked thoughtfully at Thomas.

"Does that mean that herbivores are more highly evolved than carnivores? After all, they don't believe in killing."

A few members of the jury laughed to themselves at the absurdity of the question.

Thomas slowly shook his head as if to jump start his thought process. "Maybe animals need to develop a conscience in order to understand that killing is wrong?"

"Oh," said Josh with a smile. "Now this is finally starting to make more sense. You believe that over time, it is possible to evolve to a point where you are capable of conscious thought. As we evolved over the centuries, so too, did our understanding of these natural laws."

"See, maybe there is hope for you all." Thomas marveled.

Josh nodded in agreement. "With the court's permission I would like to show a quick little video."

"Objection," said Jeremy – "Relevance?"

"Once again, your honor, because my clients are on trial for their beliefs and the plaintiffs claim that evolution is a much more plausible argument than that of God, I would like to use this video clip to help the jury understand how this argument is actually very illogical."

"I'm not certain exactly where you are going with this," declared Justice Hayden, "but I'm going to allow it. I must warn you councilor, if it is your intention to challenge the plaintiff's beliefs, then I will extend them the same courtesy."

"I understand your honor." Josh affirmed.

"Then you may proceed," said Justice Hayden.

Josh hit the remote and the flat screen on the wall came to life. It was a panoramic view of the African savannah. As the camera slowly zoomed in, a solitary zebra came into focus. It appeared to be happily snacking away on some tasty grass shoots. A fly buzzed by his head and his ear twitched a bit. As he appeared to be enjoying his morning breakfast, he was completely oblivious to the lion hiding less than twenty yards away in a patch of tall grass. As the zebra was munching away, the lioness was ever so slowly, creeping towards its prey. Once it had covered roughly one third of that distance, the lioness released all tension that had been stored up in her hind legs and she sprang into action. The nearby birds sensing danger, as if to sound the alarm immediately flew away in unison: but it was too late. The zebra lifted its head up and a look of sheer terror washed over him. His legs immediately kicked into action, jolting his body to the left. Instinct took over and the zebra realizing that danger was near: tried to outmaneuver the lioness by quickly changing directions. The lioness was not to be outsmarted, and quickly closed the gap. Once she was within reach, with a quick swipe of her powerful paw she tripped up the zebra.

Just as the lion was about to clamp down on the zebra's neck, Josh hit the remote and the screen went dark.

"I will spare the court the rest of the gory details as I am certain that you all can imagine what happens next." Josh turned to face the jury and then looked back at Thomas on the witness stand. "As you are picturing the scenario, I want to ask you this one question. Was it wrong for that lion to kill the zebra?"

"No," Thomas said smugly. "That's simply a matter of self-preservation."

"Are you trying to tell this court that the lion killed the zebra in self-defense?" Josh said smiling to himself.

A few giggles came from the jury box.

"No of course not," said Thomas. "It is a matter of survival. The lion killed the zebra for food."

"Are you trying to insinuate that if I were to kill you, it would be perfectly acceptable so long as I ate you afterwards?" Josh teased, causing a few members of the jury to chuckle out loud.

"No, as I stated before," Thomas said, trying to regain control of the conversation, "we have evolved to a point where we recognize that killing is wrong."

"Oh, I think I understand your beliefs," Josh paused as if trying to think. "If I were to kill you, it would be wrong because you have a right to live."

"Yes" Thomas snapped, getting a little frustrated with this line of questioning.

"But what about the zebra snacking on the grass, didn't he have a right to live? Maybe we should bring the lion up on murder charges?"

The jury was becoming a bit more relaxed at this point as they were finding humor in this cross-examination.

"But that's what lions do." Thomas said defensively.

"But as a civilized society, shouldn't we protect the defenseless zebra?"

"It is simply the way nature works, survival of the fittest," said Thomas falling right into his trap.

"So what you would like this jury to believe is that for millions and millions of years every single creature on this planet has been following the rules of evolution: survival of the fittest, and at some point we, human beings, have evolved so much so that the rules of evolution no longer apply to us?"

"I didn't say that." Thomas said almost defensively.

"Okay," Josh continued, "but you've already acknowledged that in nature killing is simply a matter of survival."

"That's correct."

"And if a male lion has to fight another lion to the death to protect his territory or his pride, he would only be doing what comes natural."

"Agreed."

"Then why shouldn't we be able to use that as a defense today?"

"I don't understand the question."

"I'm sorry let me rephrase it for you," Josh offered. "If I wanted to mate with a particular woman but she happens to be married, why shouldn't I, being an animal, be able to kill her husband so that I might have my way with her?"

"Because that's not the way things work in a civilized society," Thomas protested.

"So what you are telling this court is that perhaps forty or fifty thousand years ago when we were still living in caves that might have been the way things worked, but since that time we have evolved to a point where we recognize that killing is wrong."

"I'd say most people recognize that killing is wrong." Thomas corrected him.

"Then please explain to this court," pleaded Josh, "why it is not considered wrong for a lion to kill a zebra?"

"That's different," Thomas remarked, as he sensed he was losing control.

"Why?"

"That is simply a matter of survival."

"So?" Josh knew he had him on the ropes now.

"If a lion kills a zebra, it is only so that it will have the nourishment to survive," Thomas pleaded.

"But If I were to kill someone so that I could take their money, it would allow me to be able to buy the nourishment needed to survive?"

"But all humans have a fundamental right to life." Thomas proclaimed.

"Don't zebras also have a fundamental right to live? See, you can't have it both ways. You cannot argue that we are exactly like every other animal on earth yet somehow we, human beings, are different."

"Why is stealing wrong?" Josh held up his hand before Thomas had a chance to answer. "In nature, everywhere you look; the strong steal from the weak. It is simply survival of the fittest."

"But we've evolved," Thomas protested, desperately trying to persuade the jury.

"So, if I am understanding you correctly, you are asking members of the jury to believe that DNA proves every species on this planet have all derived from the same single-celled organism. Then according to your theory, through a series of genetic mutations, we have evolved to the point where we are today- over 8 million different species of plants and animals, all following the same basic guidelines of natural selection which is to say - survival of the fittest. That is, of course, except human beings. Are you really implying that you believe that we have evolved to such a high degree that survival of the fittest no longer applies? That's your argument? Don't you understand what a contradiction that is?"

Although he was reluctant to admit it, Thomas could feel the logic behind his side of the exchange rapidly slipping away. "It's hard to explain," he said, hoping this answer would suffice.

Josh knew that the plaintiff's attorney would probably vocalize an objection but he decided to try and sneak it in anyway.

Josh turned to face the jury. "It all comes back to beliefs. My clients choose to believe in God because after looking at all the evidence, this is what makes the most sense to them. You get to choose what makes the most sense to you. Either we are exactly like all other animals and we should be governed by the same rules of survival or we are different. And if we are different, what sets us apart?"

Josh breathed a heavy sigh of relief as he heard no objections and turned back to face Thomas. He gently rested his finger on his upper lip as if to momentarily think about his next line of attack. "No more questions for this witness your honor."

Justice Hayden glanced over towards the clock and divulged, "Now seems like a pretty good time to wrap things up for the weekend. Mr. Mendoza you will be allowed to redirect your witness when we resume on Monday.

After the jury was dismissed and Justice Hayden had walked back into his chambers, Clare leaned in towards Josh. "Are we still thinking about retreating Mr. Randall?"

"Today wasn't so bad, but we are still a long way from where we need to be," said Josh.

"I understand that," Clare acknowledged, "but at least it feels like we are finally moving in the right direction."

"Like I think I mentioned before Mrs. Robinson, it's a process, one step at a time. We've still got a very busy day ahead of us on Monday and we are not out of the woods by any stretch of the imagination. I just want you guys to relax and try not to think about the trial for the weekend."

"I think we can do that Mr. Randall," Adam cheerfully agreed.

On second thought," Josh paused and scribbled an address down on a piece of paper. "I was wondering if you could meet me here at 11 am on Sunday."

"We normally go to church at that time," exclaimed Clare in disbelief, annoyed that he would even think about scheduling a meeting on a Sunday.

"I'm sure you guys could go to an earlier service," Josh said, trying his best to be helpful.

Clare looked at Adam with pleading eyes hoping to see if her husband might be able to help her think of a polite way to decline the offer. When he shrugged his shoulders, she understood that the situation was basically hopeless and she agreed that they would meet up with him.

"I promise," Josh said with a smile, "it won't be as painful as you think."

a peace offering

Like a golfer practicing his swing, Josh tried to go over any missteps he may have made today in court and there was nothing glaring that he could remember. Despite Clare's earlier anxiety, all in all, he surmised: it went rather smoothly. Time to decompress, he thought to himself and turned on some music.

Even though the traffic was a little bit heavy, everything was moving at a decent clip. The stereo was rocking some "Scarlet Begonias" and for the time being, all was right with the world.

"...once in a while you get shown the light..."

The music paused mid verse, as his car's Bluetooth alerted him to an incoming phone call.

"Hello" Josh said into the air.

"Glad I caught you Josh, it's Becky."

"Why Ms. Dimitri, what a pleasant surprise, to what do I owe the pleasure?"

"I was going over the Dominguez case; I'd like to get this one off my desk. Since your client has no priors, the state would be willing to reduce the charges to simple possession, two years unsupervised probation with stipulation that he complete mandatory court sanctioned drug and alcohol treatment."

"Wow, that's quite a generous offer. Why the sudden change of heart?"

"Like I said, no priors and I'd like to get this one cleared off my calendar."

"While I can appreciate the fact that you want to give him a break, let's be honest here... You know what I think... I think you and I both know that the search was bogus and the judge is going to toss it out once I drop by with a motion to suppress."

Becky sighed into the phone.

"However," Josh continued, "I think I can get my client to agree on a couple of conditions. First, I'd like it dropped from two years to one; and once he completes his probation, I want to be able to get his record expunged. He's a good kid Becky, I don't want this to haunt him the rest of his life."

"I can live with that, but please let me know as soon as possible. Oh, she said almost as an afterthought. "Have a great weekend."

"You too. I'll get you an answer by Monday." Josh said, as he hung up the phone. He smiled and thought to himself, all is as it should be, and the music cranked back to life.

"...in the strangest of places if you look at it right"

let there be light

In a mildly pleasant tone, the receptionist announced over the intercom that Paco had a visitor. He seemed a bit stunned when he came around the corner and saw Josh sitting on the couch.

"What brings you here on a Saturday?"

"Nice to see you too, Paco."

"Sorry, that came out the wrong way. Good to see you Josh."

"Morning little buddy," Josh stood and swallowed him up in a huge bear hug.

Paco did his best to remain upbeat.

"How are you holding up?" Josh asked, not wanting to give him the good news too soon.

"It's been a hectic couple of days around here," Paco said with a heavy heart.

"Why? What's going on?" Josh could sense the sadness in his voice.

"Remember last time you were here I was telling you about this girl Nikki, the one who was a cutter?"

Paco had never mentioned her name before but Josh remembered the story. "It rings a bell."

"Well, they found her Thursday morning," Paco said, trying his best to remain stoic. "Apparently she succeeded in her mission."

"Oh my God," Josh said as he felt the blood drain from his face. "I'm so sorry to hear that Paco."

"Me too," Paco divulged, as his eyes started to tear up.

"Were you guys close?"

"As close as you can be in a place like this. The thing that really sucks is even though she talked about how much she hated her life; I never really thought that she'd go through with it. I don't think anybody here did." Paco choked back the tears. "Stupid kid was only 17 years old."

"I'm so sorry. I can only imagine the pain she must have been in," Josh said honestly.

"Why does life have to be so unfair?" Paco wondered aloud.

"I wish I had a good answer for you but I don't. Sometimes terrible things just happen."

"At least she's at peace now."

"I hope you are right, Paco."

Paco could hear the sadness in his friend's voice. "But you said there is a God?"

"I believe so, yes," said Josh. "But I think that you have to want to be with Him."

"I don't get it," Paco said, becoming even more confused about the situation.

"Unfortunately, I feel that's a mistake that a lot of people make when someone they love dies. They automatically think that they are with God. Let's just say that I believe that God loves us so much that He gives us the freedom to do whatever we want in this life including giving us the option to decide how we get to spend eternity. It is a choice we all have to make. If we want nothing to do with God in this life, what makes you think that He would want to force us to spend eternity with Him?"

Josh hesitated for a moment so that he could come up with a good illustration. "Since you like to party, I want you to imagine the best possible party in the history of the world. The best music, the best beverages, the best food, the most entertaining guests... Would you rather learn about it beforehand and be given an invitation or hear about it after the fact?"

"Well, that's a stupid question."

"Precisely my point. I want you to think about Heaven in the exact same way. You have to decide where you would like to spend eternity while you are still alive... if you have convinced yourself that you have the option of waiting until after you die to choose, you've already missed the boat."

"But that doesn't make any sense," Paco protested. "If He's a loving God, why wouldn't He want everyone to be in Heaven?"

"I believe He does, but I also believe that He loves us so much that He would never force us to do anything against our will."

Josh thought about it for a moment and he came up with an example he thought might help.

"How long have you Tatiana been together?" he asked.

"Almost three years now."

"And you love her right?"

"Of course."

"Imagine if she decided that she was no longer in love with you and she wanted to go her own way."

"Dude, what the hell are you trying to say?" Paco demanded in a somewhat frightened voice.

"Relax, it's nothing like that, this is just a mental exercise."

"Don't mess with my head like that," Paco implored.

"But if she wanted to leave you," Josh continued, "do you think things would get better if you chained her up in your basement and refused to let her go?"

"Of course not, she'd be pissed."

"And rightly so," Josh agreed. "You understand that you can never force anyone to be with you. I guess I like to think about God in the very same way. The truth is, that a loving God would never force you to do anything against your will. Imagine if you were to keep Tatiana locked up... If she didn't want to be with you, do you really think you could beat her senseless or put a gun to her head and command her to love you?"

"That would be idiotic," Paco affirmed.

"Absolutely," said Josh. "Okay, so you understand that you cannot force someone to love you, but let me ask you - do you think that she would know you existed?"

"How could she not?"

"I concur. The point I am trying to make here, is that believing that you exist, is not the same thing as wanting to be with you."

"I kinda think I understand what you are trying to say."

"The way I see it," said Josh emphatically, "if there really is a God, you have to make a conscious choice that you want to be with Him."

"So what happened to Nikki?"

"I can't say for certain, but I pray that she made her peace with God." Josh answered as honestly as he could.

"But how can you know for certain that there is a God?"

"You're asking me my beliefs so I am telling you. I'm a Christian because I believe that Jesus is who He says He is and I've put my trust in Him. That's all. It doesn't make me a better person and it certainly doesn't make me any smarter. I simply believe that if you really examine all the evidence, it points to the fact there has to be a God, and Jesus is definitely His Son."

"But how can you say that? I look around and see what a shitty mess the world is and I think the exact opposite."

"It's hard to argue with that kind of logic, my friend. I can honestly see your point. It is easy to become cynical when you look at the sorry state the world is in. I know this may sound a bit strange, but for me it is actually proof that there is a God."

Paco gave him that stupid, deer in the headlights look. "What the hell are you talking about?"

"Have you ever heard people talk about the slogan - if you love something set it free...?"

"Yeah," Paco readily agreed.

"Well, I happen to believe that God loves us so much that He gives us freewill. He gives us the freedom to do whatever we want with our lives. We get to choose whatever path we desire. Sadly, some people choose to pull as far away from God as they possibly can. When people decide to live their lives as if they never have to answer for their actions; more often than not there are terrible consequences. Take Nikki's stepdad. Do you really think he cared if his actions were hurting his step daughter? All he cared about was satisfying his own disgusting and depraved desires. When you ratchet it up to the extremes, you get people like Hitler who want to impose their own sick views on the world and it doesn't matter to them, how many people they hurt along the way."

Paco gave a deep sigh and thought about his friend.

"I think," Josh continued, "that when people have so much hate in their heart, they become immune to the pain they are causing. The truth is that we live in a broken world. If God gives us free will, it is only logical that some people would do bad things that end up causing a lot of misery."

"It still doesn't make a lot of sense to me," Paco confided.

"Remember when I dropped you off here, I said that deep down inside we were all searching for something?"

"Vaguely."

"This may sound a little strange, but this life is only temporary and it is not really where we belong. Deep down inside I believe everyone knows this and, on some level, we are all searching for something more meaningful. Sadly, many of us take refuge in earthly solutions. That's why I think drugs and alcohol are so alluring. The best way I can explain it is that we are trying to recapture a feeling that we know exists, but we can barely remember. Even though you may not understand it now, what we are literally missing is LOVE. I'm not talking about the watered-down version that we might be lucky enough to experience here in this lifetime. What I'm trying to describe is a love so perfect, that it can only come from God. Once you've experienced the real thing, everything else pales in comparison."

"That's pretty trippy"

"Indeed. Look at it this way," Josh said. "For the sake of argument, let's say that I believe in God and you do not."

"I guess a more accurate way to put it would be more like I'm still on the fence." Paco volunteered.

"That's good to hear; at least you have an open mind. I can live with that for now. Imagine that I spend my entire life believing that there is a God and I am wrong. What have I really lost?" Josh asked in earnest.

"I guess you've lost the ability to experience all that life has to offer," Paco said mischievously.

"How so?"

"Well, doesn't the bible have a list of stuff you can't do?

"Let's say," Josh stipulated, "that the bible teaches some very valuable lessons on life. But for sake of argument, I can see how some people might interpret it as a list of do's and don'ts..."

"See," said Paco defiantly, "But I get to do whatever I want."

"Such as...?" Josh prodded.

"I can get drunk if I want," Paco smiled at the thought.

"Really? That's the argument you're going to use for not wanting to believe in God. You can get drunk if you want. Why not ratchet it up a notch and say you get to smoke crack and have sex with five-dollar hookers?"

Paco did his best to pretend to look horrified.

Josh continued, "what if God loves you in spite of all the rotten things you've ever thought or done? God loves everyone, even drunks and drug addicts. I happen to believe that there is absolutely nothing you can do that would make God stop loving you. He might be disgusted at some of your actions but that wouldn't make Him love you any less. I don't think believing in God means that you have to lose out on all that life has to offer. I'd say just the opposite – it enhances it."

"How could it possibly enhance life?" Paco asked in total disbelief.

"Believing in God doesn't mean that you become a robot. I get to experience all the same feelings and emotions that you do: the only real difference is that no matter what happens or what circumstance I may face in this lifetime I can take comfort in the fact that when I eventually die, I get to spend eternity with the God of the Universe."

"But what about all the list of things you can't do?" Paco demanded.

"Let's say that I believe the bible gives you a blueprint as to how you should live your life. If you choose not to follow the suggestions you are probably going to have a much bumpier road. You are not forced to do anything. No one can force you to remain sober, but if you decide to spend every waking moment getting drunk, I suspect that it might eventually cause some serious problems. I guess it is all a matter of how you prefer to look at things. Even though I may not comprehend exactly why; I believe that there are, as you call them, 'rules' which are in place for our own good."

Paco stared at his friend intently.

Josh continued, "Think about a little kid, maybe a two or three-year-old. He or she doesn't know enough about how the world works to understand everything. If you were to tell them not to play in the road, they might find your 'rules' annoying. The truth of the matter, is that as an adult, you understand that even though there may not be any cars in the street at the present moment, you know that if a car came speeding around the corner the results could be disastrous."

Paco nodded his head.

"So, as an adult you can understand things that a child might not grasp. Well, if you think about God, everything gets magnified on a much larger scale. I simply accept that God is able to see things from a much different perspective, that's all. Do I think that doing drugs is dead end path? Absolutely. Do I think you can have a better life without them? Unequivocally."

"But..." Yet again, Paco tried to object.

Josh held up his hand and continued, "Imagine that God only wants the very best for you. He wants you to be happy. But He also understands that there are certain behaviors that might not be good for you and will eventually have unintended consequences. Even though you may not understand it now, perhaps someday it might make sense."

"It's a lot to digest," Paco divulged.

"I know it is a lot to take in, I guess I tend to see the world in black and white – right and wrong. But sometimes the world can be a very confusing place."

"How so?"

"I don't understand how some people can possibly think that truth is merely subjective. Sadly, I actually have a very intelligent friend who says *"well that's your truth."* For me, something is either true or it is not. There is no other alternative."

"But isn't everyone entitled to their beliefs?" Paco speculated.

"You are absolutely right," Josh agreed. "You even have the right to believe that the moon is made of blue cheese if you like, but it doesn't make it any more real. Think about this: imagine if the district attorney accused you of killing Abraham Lincoln. Imagine if she had you arrested and brought you to trial. You bring out all these witnesses to prove that Lincoln was killed more than one hundred and thirty years before you were born. What if she tried to use the argument ... *"well, it is true for me?"* Don't you think she would be laughed right out of court because everyone would understand that she has lost touch with reality?"

"More like... they'd know she was nuttier than a squirrel's turd." Paco said, as he laughed at the image.

"However, once you take God out of the equation, I can see how people might argue that there is no definitive truth or 'right' and 'wrong'. Everything would be a matter of opinion. How can one opinion be more right than another?"

Paco shrugged his shoulders.

"Here's a good example," Josh offered. "You know the nineteen hijackers who flew the planes into the World Trade Center on September 11th?

"Not personally." Paco said, smiling.

Josh tried to conceal his smile and trudged on. "All nineteen of those Islamic jihadists believed that they were following the truth. Just because you believe something with absolute conviction, doesn't automatically mean that it is true. They went to their graves fully convinced that they were right. If there is no God, how can you argue that they were wrong?"

"Because the people in those buildings didn't want to die, killing people is just wrong." Paco protested.

"So what I think you are trying to say," Josh deduced, "is that you believe it was wrong for the jihadists to impose their will on others?"

"Absolutely."

"I'm happy that we can agree that killing thousands of innocent people is wrong," Josh said. "But the way I see it, if there is no God that means it is up to the people in charge, the actual governments, to decide what they consider to be right and wrong."

"Exactly, that's why we have laws."

"Okay," Josh reasoned, "Let me put it to you another way. It is easy to argue that societies have laws in place to protect its citizens. Stealing is wrong...don't get caught. Rape is wrong ... don't get caught. Murder is wrong...don't get caught. Are you following me so far?"

"Yeah, I'm still following you." Paco humored him.

"You can use the laws of our society to define what you feel is right or wrong, but that doesn't always work," Josh speculated. "Two hundred years ago, in our country slavery was legal. Did that make it right?"

It only took a brief second for Paco to say "No."

"In the seventeen and eighteen hundreds the United States government stole land from the Native Americans and pushed them onto reservations. Was it right for us to steal their land?"

"No."

"Seventy-five years ago, in Nazi Germany, Jews were considered to be less than human. When a guard in a concentration camp decided to kill a Jew, there were no penalties or repercussions. If Hitler had won the war, do you think any of those guards would have been brought to trial for murder?"

"I doubt it," Paco acknowledged.

"Well," Josh speculated, "were the actions of the guards morally right or wrong?"

"Of course, they were wrong."

"See what I mean. Not every society shares the exact same values. How can someone argue that there is an ultimate "right" and "wrong" if they are only going by the rules of the local government? There are many governments today that do not share our same value system. For something to be universally wrong; such as murder, doesn't it make sense that these "laws" must exist outside the government?"

"I guess," Paco mumbled.

"Look, there are only two real choices, either there is such a thing as truth or there is not. If truth does exist, where does it come from? We, human beings, are constantly trying to manipulate one another for our own personal advantage. That's what we do. Anyone who says that they have never deceived another person, is lying to themselves. If every single human being has lied at one time or another, does is really make sense that truth is a man-made concept? We both know that truth does exist; doesn't it make sense to seek out the source? Unfortunately, there are some very smart people who are way too stubborn to actually take the time to search for the answers."

Paco paused to think about what Josh was saying.

"It really doesn't matter how many different arguments I use to try to help you understand that there is a God, nothing will make sense unless you decide for yourself that you want to learn about Him. I want to switch subjects for a moment," Josh said. "Let me ask you... If there really was a God, do you think He would have the right to punish us for our misdeeds? Let's use Hitler as an example. Would a perfect and Holy God have a right to be upset with Hitler's actions?"

"I suppose so,"

"That's it? Just... I suppose so?" Josh looked at his friend in disbelief and shook his head.

"Okay. Here's something to contemplate. I want you to imagine that there really is a God and He has the right to judge you, how comfortable would you feel if you had to argue that you lived a perfect life?"

"What do you mean by perfect?"

"Exactly what it sounds like – absolutely perfect. Never lied, never stolen, never cheated, not even a single dirty thought."

"I'm screwed," Paco confessed. "That ship sailed a long, long time ago."

"We pretty much all are," Josh said. "Now I want to envision that you are on trial and you find yourself standing before the judge. In order to go free, you have to have lived an absolutely perfect life. If, however, you can't prove you've lived a perfect life... you get the death penalty."

Just the thought of it, sent an involuntary shiver down Paco's spine.

"Now here comes the best part, imagine that there is an attorney who will happily offer up His services for free... but there is a catch; He is only able to help you if you are willing to put your trust in Him. Let me back that up for a second. I almost forgot the most important detail. He can guarantee you will be found not-guilty because He has been given the power to wipe your record clean. Not only that, but He also has the authority to give you a full and absolute pardon for any possible crimes you might commit in the future."

"That sounds almost too good to be true.

"I can see how you might think that, but it's not very complicated. If you want to be forgiven, all you need to do is ask. I'm quite confident that God would be okay with me saying this," Josh pointed out. "If you still have lingering doubts, simply try and prove Him wrong! If Jesus isn't really who He claims to be, then it should be pretty simple to expose. If you want, you can even think of this as a dare. I urge you to accept the challenge, I can assure you that you've got nothing to lose and everything to gain. All I can say is that once you come to understand that there actually is an all loving God who is with you every step of the way, it becomes so much easier to want to put your trust in Him. Just in case you might be tempted to think that I'm making all this stuff up... trust me, I'm not that smart. All you have to do is ask around. Most of my closest friends will happily attest to this fact."

Paco took a moment to gather his thoughts and meditate on what Josh was telling him.

"It's been a long day Paco, and I know you've got a lot on your mind with what happened to your friend Nikki and all. Please don't misunderstand me, I am not trying to force you to do anything... but I am begging you to take this seriously. I totally get it, when it comes to religion, there are some very scary people out there. However, just because there are a few complete nutjobs in this world doesn't mean you should ignore the truth. I know this may be hard for you to swallow, but what if God could take whatever you are going through and use it to His advantage? Sometimes terrible things happen, but I do believe that God can use circumstances to get our attention."

"Get our attention?" Paco repeated the words as if it might help him understand.

"I think God is always trying to get our attention." Josh explained. "I think we just get so caught up in the day to day trappings of life, that we miss the signals. As implausible as it may sound, how do you know that God isn't using this conversation to try to reach you right at this very moment?"

Paco thought about what his friend was saying, but said nothing.

"The truth is out there, Paco. You just have to make the conscious decision whether or not you want to follow it. I wish I could give you a better answer but this is a choice you're going to have to make for yourself. I don't want you to simply take my word for it. If there really is a God and He is offering you the gift of eternity, don't you think it might be a good idea to at least do your own research before you decide to turn your back on Him?"

"Maybe," Paco said, "but aren't you putting all your eggs in one basket?"

"Absolutely. And for the record, I'm glad you finally noticed. When you take the time to think about it; the average lifespan here on earth is what, maybe 75-80 years?"

"I guess."

"Well, consider the age of the universe. If I were to use the analogy of comparing this lifetime to accumulating money, it would be like saying you place more value on 75 cents than becoming a billionaire. It isn't very logical. Why would anyone want to leave eternity (which is way more valuable than money) up to chance? Wouldn't most sane, rational people want to know the truth? By the same token, if it is indeed the truth, you have to be able to examine it from every single angle and it will still make perfect sense."

Paco shrugged his shoulders.

"I suspect that everyone would like to think that their beliefs are true. For this to be the case, one must acknowledge that no one's beliefs can be better than another. Hitler believed in a master race and he was destined to rule the world. He was more than willing to destroy anyone or anything that got in his way. If everyone's beliefs are equal, how can you say that his actions were wrong?"

"I'm not sure."

"I submit to you, it's because your conscience tells you otherwise. I suppose that there are probably some unscrupulous people who might be inclined to argue that robbing a bank or committing murder is simply the equivalent of going faster than the posted speed limit when driving a car. It is only wrong if you get caught. The reality is that when you take God out of the equation, getting caught is all that matters. I think it all comes back to good and evil, right and wrong. It seems perplexing to me that if there is no such thing as God and we truly lived in a cold and impersonal universe, why would these concepts even exist?

"Maybe," Paco offered, "they are simply opposites that occur in nature such as hot and cold, light and dark, good and evil."

"I like the way you think," Josh acknowledged. "But there is one major problem with that logic. If there is no driving force behind the universe, then ask yourself why one would be preferential over another? To say that they are both equal is absurd. Imagine this scenario... A pretty, young teenage girl is driving home alone and her car breaks down on a deserted road. A stranger stops by and offers her a ride. He goes out of his way and brings her directly to her parent's doorstep and patiently waits until she is safely inside. Don't you think that most sane, rational people would agree that his actions qualify as good?"

Paco thought about his friend Nikki, nodded his head and replied "sure."

"Now imagine that instead of driving her home, this same stranger drags the girl into the woods and repeatedly rapes her before torturing and then killing her. Only a sociopath would hesitate to consider his actions evil. Keep in mind that because the stranger has freewill, he has the option to consider either action. The very fact that these actions are not equal is a strong indication that there is some sort of driving force behind the universe and that force is definitely ... GOOD."

Josh continued... "Some people may claim that putting your faith in God is as foolish as believing in Santa Claus or the Tooth Fairy. They are certainly entitled to their beliefs. In addition to what atheists and agnostics may subscribe to, there are also many different religions all claiming to have a monopoly on the truth. The real question is – who do you want to trust?"

Paco thought about it for a moment and then blurted out, "what about reincarnation?"

"That's a pretty good point. However, if you think about it logically, aren't you just adding layers?"

"What do you mean by layers?"

"When you boil it all down, once you die there can only be one of two possible choices. After you die, there is either some sort of afterlife or there is not."

"So?" Paco interjected.

"Let's say you believe in reincarnation and you think this could be your fiftieth or even your hundredth different lifetime. You have to concede that at some point you are going to die and move on to the 'next level'. Are you following me so far?"

With a nod of his head, he assured Josh that he was keeping up.

"Well if there is an afterlife, then doesn't reincarnation conveniently absolve you of the responsibility for your actions here in this life? Why would the choices you make in this lifetime make any difference, if you knew you could simply make different choices in your next life?"

"I guess I never really took the time to think about it that way."

"It's okay, you're not alone. If you think about it rationally, it is impossible to have dozens of different religions, each with a completely different set of instructions, all leading to the exact same place."

"And what would that place be?"

"For lack of a better word, let's call it Heaven. It all comes down to one simple point. Either there is some sort of afterlife or there is not. As I mentioned before, if this life is all we get, one could make a pretty good argument for doing exactly as you pleased and if it is illegal, just don't get caught. But if there is some sort of afterlife, doesn't it make sense to choose the right path? Think about it this way, if there really is a God that created the universe, doesn't that mean he also created everything in it?"

"So what's your point?"

"Can you really imagine wanting to follow a vindictive god that actually hated much of his own creation? Doesn't it seem a bit suspicious that a loving god would leave behind a 'holy book' that inspires his followers to kill non-believers?"

"It seems a bit sketchy to me."

"I couldn't possibly agree more. Doesn't it make much more sense to follow a compassionate and caring God that loves you in spite of all your faults? A God that loves you so much that He wants to give you the gift of eternity. There is absolutely nothing you can do to earn your way to heaven, this is a free gift – but you have to be willing to accept it. Being a Christian does not mean that you will instantly become a better person or your life will miraculously turn out to be perfect. It doesn't even imply that you will never do anything wrong in the future. It simply means that you understand that Jesus died for you sins, and you are willing to put your trust in Him so that your sins will no longer be counted against you. End of story."

"I think," Josh continued, "that the reason so many Christians may seem overzealous about their faith is that they understand that the stakes are far too important. It all circles back to freewill. I realize I'm probably repeating myself but if you want absolutely nothing to do with God in this lifetime, why would an All Loving God want to force you to spend eternity with Him? By the way, God isn't waiting for you to be perfect to come to Him, He loves you as you are."

"I just don't understand how you can be so certain."

"Do you really think you're the first person on this planet to have reservations about God? I've got news for you. You're not the only skeptic out there, but let me ask you a question... Do you trust me?"

"What are you talking about?"

"I want you to consider this. Why on earth would someone that you love and trust deliberately want to give you advice that would be harmful to you? Do you really think I am telling you all this because I am secretly trying to screw you over?"

"No, of course not."

"Since I am the one who is currently attempting to give you this information, even if you don't completely subscribe to what I am saying... ask yourself why would I be expending so much energy trying to convince you that something was true, if I honestly knew that it was really a lie and it would somehow prevent you from enjoying a happy life?"

"I'd like to believe you probably wouldn't."

"Exactly! I realize that this might seem a bit far-fetched, but how do you know that God hasn't actually entrusted me with the task of helping you understand the truth about Him?"

"Seriously?"

"Yup. I'm hoping that someday, this will all become abundantly clear. Perhaps I've given you enough information that, at the very least, it has piqued your curiosity. As soon as you have a sincere desire to know the truth, I'm quite confident that you will end up finding it. This is your life my friend; there are no absolutely limitations as to what you can accomplish once you set your mind to it. By the same token, you are also free to live it any way you want to. The best I can do," Josh stressed, "is to help point you in the right direction. The rest is up to you."

"Oh I almost forgot," Josh said, in an absentminded way, "I was actually coming up here to give you some good news."

"Good news?"

"The D.A. offered you a plea bargain. The state is willing to reduce the possession with intent charges down to a simple possession."

"What does that mean?"

"For starters," Josh reckoned, "it means you won't have to worry about any jail time."

"I thought you said we could get that one thrown out?" Paco protested.

"There's a good chance we can, but she agreed to just one year of probation."

"What do you think?" Paco asked, hoping his friend would tell him what to do.

Josh didn't want to let him know that it was unsupervised probation and it meant that he probably wouldn't even have to worry about doing monthly pee tests. Josh knew that it was probably better for Paco if he thought that the court system would force him to stay clean.

"You really don't have a lot of time to waste holding out for a better offer. Chances are you will get the same probation deal for the drunk driving anyway so you're not losing any ground. I've got it worked out that as long as you stay out of trouble, we can get this wiped off you record."

"Do I have to give an answer now?" Paco inquired, stalling for more time to think about it.

"Nope, but I told her I'd let her know on Monday. It's a good offer Paco, but I get it, it's your decision to make."

Josh stood up to get ready to leave.

"Thanks for stopping by Josh, I really am glad you came. And thanks again for all your help."

"Is there anything I can get for you?" Josh offered.

"Nah," said Paco, "Like you said I can do this standing on my head. And for the record, what you were saying kinda made sense."

"Just kinda?"

"Now you are just being greedy," Paco smiled back.

"Are you all set with a ride next Thursday?"

"Yeah, Tatiana's coming to get me."

"And then what?"

"I'm not on a mission to get trashed if that's what you're hinting at."

"That's a good start Paco, at this point, that's a very good start. I'm going to clue you in on a little secret. You'll have a much happier life if you don't sweat the small stuff."

Josh let his eyes dart about the room scanning every nook and cranny to make certain that no one was snooping around to hear what he was about to say next and then whispered in Paco's ear. "In the grand scheme of things ... it's all small stuff." With that, he winked and swallowed his friend up in a giant bear hug.

Josh was almost at the door when Paco called out.

"Oh, I almost forgot," he said with curiosity. "They don't allow random visitors here, how come you get to pop in whenever you like?"

"Being an attorney has its privileges my friend." Josh said over his shoulder, as he waved goodbye and headed back to his car.

my sheep hear my voice

Josh arrived to see Adam and Clare standing on the sidewalk outside the rough cut, stone, turn of the century church which looked quite out of place amongst the steel and glass buildings of downtown Denver. As the three of them approached the old building, Josh looked quite astonished to see his good friend Matt standing at the entryway.

"I see they've got you working the door today." Josh said, as if it were totally out of the ordinary.

"Just trying to make myself useful," Matt replied with a warm smile.

"I can appreciate that," said Josh, and then added for good measure, "Are you staying out of trouble?"

"You'd be the first to know." Matt acknowledged as he winked at him.

"Then I'll take that as a yes."

Clare and Adam were momentarily taken aback; they were a bit puzzled as to how Josh could be on such good terms with someone who looked as though they obviously had spent a lifetime on the wrong side of the law.

"You're looking well my friend."

"How very kind of you to notice," Josh said jokingly. "Matt, these are a couple of good friends of mine, this is Adam and his beautiful wife Clare."

Adam offered his hand and it was immediately swallowed up in Matt's meaty paw. "Welcome, we're happy that you could make it. And for the record, any friend of Josh's is a friend of mine. If you have any questions or I can be of any assistance, please don't hesitate to let me know."

With that, Matt turned to greet the next batch of arrivals.

Clare looked around and smiled to herself. Everyone appeared to be so friendly despite the fact that it looked as though it could have been a homeless shelter mixed in with a Hell's Angels convention. Obviously, there isn't a dress code here, she thought to herself.

As they were conversing in the foyer, Clare heard the opening chords and immediately recognized the song;

although she could never recall hearing it in a church setting before.

Once inside, the atmosphere was almost electric. Never in her life had she seen an entire congregation so moved by music.

After the musicians had finished their set and left the stage, Clare did a double take as she saw the big burly biker from the door, walk up to the podium at the center of the stage.

"Good Morning, how's everyone doing today? For those of you who may be new here my name is Pastor Matt, and I would like to thank you for coming."

"I'm sure most of you have probably heard the news today about what happened last night in Orlando. I think it is only appropriate that we should start off with a prayer for the victims and their families."

"Father, I want to thank you for gathering each of us safely here today. In such troubling times, dear Lord, our hearts go out to the people of Orlando. Not just for the victims but also for the friends and family members who have lost loved ones. We pray that you comfort them in their time of sorrow. The Bible tells us that God is sovereign over all events in life, both good and bad and it also tells us that God uses all things for His glory."

"Dear Lord, please use me as an instrument to help others hear your voice. Although we may not understand the exact reason why everything happens in this world, we trust in your unending love and faithfulness. Give us the strength to reach out to those who are suffering, and help guide us to become a source of inspiration to those in their hour of need. We pray this in your name Lord Jesus, Amen"

Immediately after finishing with the opening prayer Pastor Matt continued, "Too often, in today's hectic world, we forget what's really important. Why are we here? I believe, with all my heart, the reason why we are born into this world is to look up. Out of all the millions and millions of choices we can make in our lives, the most important decision we will ever make ... We must decide whether or not we want to spend eternity with God."

"That being said, for those of us who have already chosen to put our trust in Jesus, as Christians, we have a duty to help others understand the truth. I believe we are here to help make heaven as crowded as possible. Not everyone will have the opportunity to read the bible in its entirety, and it is quite likely that you may be the only glimpse of Jesus that some people will ever see. If you sincerely want to help change the world, it all starts here." Matt gently thumped his heart. "Don't let the absence of perfection be the enemy of the good. I think it would be extremely sad to get to heaven and realize that nobody was there as a direct result of your actions. If you are really taking your faith seriously, shouldn't you want to help others understand the truth? Here's a news flash, if you are not part of the solution, then you are actually part of the problem."

"For those of us who already know that following Christ is the answer; we all have a simple choice to make. Imagine what could be accomplished if everyone hearing these words... actually decided to focus their complete attention on helping even just one person understand the truth about God. And how would you go about achieving this goal? The solution to this puzzle is remarkably easy. It all comes back to LOVE."

Pastor Matt slowly walked to the edge of the stage and continued with his sermon.

"You could spend a lifetime attempting to learn everything Jesus was trying to teach us and still not scratch the surface. Today, I'd like to concentrate on Luke 15:11, the parable about the prodigal son. For those of you who are not familiar; this is the story about the wayward son who demanded that his father immediately give him all of his inheritance, which he then proceeded to recklessly squander away on booze and loose women. Imagine for a moment, that this was your child. Would you have a right to feel hurt or angry? I know that I would..."

"But the story continues, once all the money was gone, the son had an epiphany and realized how badly he has screwed up. He then decided to go back and beg for his father's forgiveness. Instead of being angry, we are told that the father saw his son from afar and ran to him. Before the son could even vocalize his apology, the father hugged him and welcomed him with open arms. So much so, that he even threw a giant party to celebrate his return. This, my friends, is unconditional love in action. I believe that one of the reasons why Jesus told this parable was to illustrate how much God loves us. It doesn't matter what we have done in this lifetime, He will still welcome us with open arms. Whether or not you choose to admit it, at one time or another, we have all turned our back on God."

"Unfortunately, we live in a broken world. We do things that hurt and annoy one another. If God is willing to forgive you for all the rotten things you've done in this lifetime, what gives you the right to be unwilling to forgive others? I shouldn't have to point this out, but there is already far too much hatred in this world. Instead of treating our fellow human beings with contempt or indifference, maybe we would have a much greater opportunity to help others understand the truth, if we responded with nothing but the same unconditional love God has shown us."

Matt reasoned, "Jesus lived His life with love and compassion. Are you? Each and every one of us must look back at the mistakes we have made, and remember where we would be without the grace of God."

Matt took a deep breath and forged ahead with the sermon.

"Last night 49 people were murdered because someone was so blinded by hatred, that they were convinced that killing these people would make their god happy. I want you to remember that the one and only, true God loves all of them, but sadly there were probably some who died before they had a chance to understand the truth. Every single person that was murdered last night, had friends and family members who are now hurting. They are crying out for answers. I believe it is our job, as Christians, to help comfort them. This brings us back to love and compassion."

"If you think about it rationally, everything you have ever done in your entire life has brought you to this very moment, right here, right now. You are a culmination of all your previous choices and actions. It really doesn't matter where you are on your spiritual journey, it is extremely important that you take the time to reflect upon these words. Short of reaching out and vigorously shaking you by the shoulders, there is little I can do to help you understand that right from the very beginning: this message was specifically designed to reach your ears. I'm sure you are all familiar with the passage... once I was blind, but now I can see. How do you know that God didn't specifically intend for you to be the eyes of the world?"

"A show of hands please. Has anyone ever made any mistakes or bad choices?"

Everyone in the congregation simultaneously raised their hands.

"I know that I have," Pastor Matt volunteered, with his hand held high. "Well, sometimes certain decisions may have lingering and far reaching consequences. Since we do not know the exact circumstances that others may have gone through, I believe that the best thing we can do for them is to give them a fresh start. Think of it this way, can you really imagine a five-year-old saying when I grow up: I want to be a junkie or a prostitute?"

"The point I am trying to make is that sometimes we get so caught up in our own little bubble that we truly forget to think about the pain and suffering others may have experienced. I'm sure almost everyone has probably encountered a homeless person who reeked of alcohol and was begging for change."

"What if that homeless person, as a child, was beaten every single day of his or her life? I want you to picture a small child crying themself to sleep because their tiny body is all black and blue and covered from head to toe with welts from getting whipped so hard with a belt. What if the only way the child learned to cope, was that they found out they could numb the pain by drinking it away? Or think about a young child that had to live every day of their life in fear because they were continuously molested. Would you think to yourself that it has to be the child's fault because they somehow must have acted seductively, or they deserved a beating because they provoked the adult to anger? I certainly hope not."

"Does God love everyone? Does that include adulterers, homosexuals, drug addicts, prostitutes and even career criminals? The answer is yes, just in case you were wondering. I believe that if we are to help others understand unconditional love, it is almost as if when we think about people; we need to reset the clock back to when they were three or four years old and still an innocent child. If you encountered a small child who was traumatized with fear, wouldn't you naturally want to cradle them in your arms and let them know everything is going to be okay?"

The words Pastor Matt spoke grabbed hold of Clare and cut deeply into her soul. She felt the warm tears rolling down her cheeks as the pastor continued with the sermon but she could no longer focus upon his words. It was the feeling that was transforming her heart, which currently consumed her. She now knew what needed to be done.

the harvest is plentiful

As they stood on the sidewalk appreciating the beautiful spring day, Josh wanted to get a feel for how they enjoyed the sermon.

"So," Josh asked, "was it as scary as you thought?"

"We," said Adam, "didn't realize you were inviting us to join you for services."

"So, what did you think?"

"Very moving," Clare honestly confessed.

Josh smiled, and took a deep breath. "I don't usually like to talk shop on Sundays, but since this case is directly relevant to God, I'd like to think He'd be willing to forgive us. Would you care to join me for a cup of coffee?"

They walked the two blocks soaking up the warmth of the sun's rays and drinking in all that the world had to offer. The coffee shop Josh chose was one of those cute, trendy new places popping up all over town; soft music playing in the background and lots of cozy chairs on which to sit upon. There was an oversized L shaped brown suede couch tucked into the corner that was calling their name.

"How you guys take your coffee?"

Josh proceeded to place the order as Adam and Clare sank into the warm, comfy sofa.

When Josh returned with the drinks he decided to jump right back into the conversation.

"I know this trial has been very stressful for you guys," Josh said. "And I want you to know that it is not too late to reverse directions."

"What do you mean reverse directions?" Clare said in almost a panic.

"It's not too late to focus our attention on winning this case."

"Remember," Clare reminded him, "when we were eating lunch last week and you suggested the possibility that maybe we could use this platform for something more important?"

"How could I forget?" Josh said, feeling a bit ashamed that he put them in this position.

"Well," Clare interjected, "Adam and I have been doing a lot of thinking."

"And praying," Adam added for good measure.

"Be that as it may," Clare said, and then lovingly smiled back at her husband. "We've come to the conclusion that you are right. Maybe it's not about winning this case."

"You do realize that you are running the risk of being ostracized. I'm not just talking about by the gay community boycotting your shop. You need to face the fact that for whatever reason, many people are not secure enough in their own beliefs to be willing to help others recognize the truth. Sadly, there are also far too many Christians who are extremely stubborn. Some are so insistent when it comes to their own personal views that they would much rather take an all or nothing approach."

"But no one should be forced to compromise their beliefs," Clare said defensively.

"I completely agree," Josh acknowledged. "But imagine a Christian who happens to be Amish approaching a non-believer and saying ... I realize you've expressed a desire to learn about the truth and I will happily explain everything I know, but before I go any further... you must first accept that God has no problem with His followers utilizing technology just so long as it was developed prior to 1815. Do you really think most sane, rational people would stick around to hear the rest of the argument?"

"Probably not."

"Unfortunately, there are some people who tend to get hung up on minutia. They would rather insist that you must accept EVERYTHING exactly as they see it right from the very beginning, instead of concentrating on the bigger picture. For me, the most important thing you can do is help someone to understand is that there really is an all loving God who wants you to spend eternity with Him."

"You make a very persuasive argument Mr. Randall," Clare said smiling.

"I hate to be the bearer of bad news, but I want you to prepare yourselves that no matter what evidence we may present in court, there is a very good chance that it will not immediately sink in. The reality is that we all learn at different speeds and some people are so hard-headed that they will simply ignore everything they hear."

"But aren't members of the jury supposed to wait until the trial is over and then deliberate on all the evidence before they make up their mind?" Adam speculated.

"Of course," Josh added. "But that doesn't mean that they will take the time to think about it next week or next month. Many people are so blinded by their own sense of self-importance that they are unwilling to admit that they might be even remotely wrong about their beliefs. It is also possible that those who are not actively seeking the truth could find this entire ordeal exceedingly repetitious and boring. I suspect that there are even some who may have been arguing to themselves, as the evidence was being presented."

"But the trial isn't over yet," Clare protested emphatically.

"I am well aware of this, but we are in a very precarious situation. No one wakes up and thinks to themself, today is the day I am going to contemplate the existence of God. You have to understand that there are some people who might not be happy about the fact that they are being compelled to tackle a subject that makes them feel uncomfortable."

"But you've already made some excellent points for the jury to think about," Clare suggested; as if she felt the need to defend him.

"Epiphanies are usually very short lived. What might make perfect sense here at this very moment, could be rendered useless if it is tucked away on the back shelf of your mind. Everything about the world we live in, screams urgency. Life is full of distractions; this will never go away."

"But," Clare reasoned, "how can you prevent them from simply glossing over what is being said?"

"That's the million-dollar question. Unfortunately, I think for most of us, we are so stubborn that too often, it takes a tragic wake-up call to bring us to our knees. Like it or not, death is an uncomfortable subject. I believe that on an intellectual level most people will acknowledge that they know this life is temporary. However, when it comes to eternity, I'm afraid that there might be a lot of people who are willing to take their chances and simply hope for the best.

Clare thought about it for a moment. "Maybe you could point out that if there is no afterlife, then everything we do in this lifetime would ultimately be meaningless."

"I'm not sure I'm following you."

"Don't you see," Clare revealed, "if this life is all we get; how can anyone argue that the way one chooses to live their life is wrong? I'm sure you've heard people use the argument that we should be allowed to do whatever makes us happy."

Josh nodded in agreement.

"Well, if we are all permitted to do exactly as we please, then how can anyone realistically argue that one way of living your life is better than another? I know you like to take things to the extremes," Clare reminded him. "Think about murder. I suspect that most people have heard of the notorious serial killer, Jack the Ripper."

"I would imagine so," Josh acknowledged.

"What if being a serial killer made Jack the Ripper happy? According to history, no one was ever held accountable for the killings – in essence – he got away with it. Now, if there is no afterlife and no eternal justice, then what difference does it really make? How could anyone say his actions were wrong?"

"That's a tricky one," Josh said, "because I think even most atheists would agree that killing people is wrong but I think I understand where you are trying to go with this subject."

Josh thought about it for a moment... "How's this for a more up to date example? Let's say I figured out a way to rob a bank electronically. If I somehow managed to steal one dollar from every single person on the planet with a bank account, I would end up becoming a multi-billionaire overnight. If I never get caught, I can have a pretty comfortable life. If there is no God and no afterlife, how could anyone possibly argue that what I did was wrong?"

"I think that's a great example," Clare proclaimed. "See, I believe that if we could get the members of the jury to think about right and wrong, maybe they would understand that there has to be some sort of eternal justice system."

Despite everything, Josh wasn't entirely satisfied. "I just wish I could think of the perfect argument."

"People aren't as naïve as you might think Mr. Randall," Clare stated succinctly.

"Convincing atheists that there is a God is monumental task." Josh reiterated. "Persuading people that the we need to put our trust in Jesus becomes much harder when every single denomination insists that they are the only ones who know the REAL truth. To a non-believer it makes it extremely hard to understand and it becomes even harder for them to know who to trust."

"Perhaps we are going about it the wrong way." Adam suggested.

"What do you mean?"

"I'm sure you've heard the expression - strength in numbers."

"Of course."

"Well, remember when you said that there were probably going to be three or four Christians on the jury. What if we could use this fact to our advantage?"

"But how could that possibly help?"

"It's really a matter of common sense," Adam said. "For the past two thousand years there have been dozens, if not hundreds, of different factions all competing to entice others. As Christians, aren't we supposed to be the adults in the room? Wouldn't we have much greater success if we concentrated all of our energy on helping non-believers, instead of wasting our time bickering amongst ourselves as to who really has a monopoly on the truth? Maybe the time has finally come for Christians to stand together."

"Don't you think." Josh surmised, "that you might be setting the bar a bit too high?"

"Just because something hasn't been done before, doesn't mean it can't be done."

"But Adam," Clare pointed out. "Not everybody believes the exact same thing. What if there are members of different denominations on the jury?"

"That's the best part." Adam speculated. "It really shouldn't make a difference if they are Catholic, Baptists or even Lutheran for that matter. This is not about insisting that the doctrines of any particular faction are wrong. But rather, imagine what could be accomplished if everyone simply focused upon the basic fundamentals, instead of getting hung up on the specific details."

"I think I get what you are trying to achieve." Josh said smiling. "If I am grasping this correctly, we should be concentrating on helping people understand that it is the things that actually unites us as Christians which are of the utmost importance."

"Exactly. As followers of Christ, there are certain beliefs that we all must share."

"Such as?" Josh prodded, trying to get Adam to elaborate.

"First and foremost, that there is a God. That God is not only loving, but Holy and just. God has a Son named Jesus. That when Jesus died on the cross, He paid the price for our sins. And most importantly, the only way to get to spend eternity with God is by trusting that Jesus did this for you."

"I think that it's a really great approach but you do realize that there is always the possibility that it may not work. Even though there probably will be Christians hearing this argument, you can't be 100% certain that anyone will want to cooperate."

"Why is that?"

"Regrettably, there are far too many followers of Christ who have adopted the attitude of ... Why should I bother? What's in it for me? People are selfish and lazy by nature and sometimes we will utilize even the flimsiest of excuses as to why we needn't help."

Upon hearing this, Adam looked a little dejected.

"Besides, I am still stumped as to how we can introduce Jesus into this court case and convince enough jury members to sway this trial in your favor."

Clare smiled. "Maybe that shouldn't be our goal. Adam and I knew the risks we were taking and we still decided to move forward. When all is said and done, you might be right. We might not immediately convince enough members of the jury to win this trial. On the other hand, what if we are successful in convincing even a single person to start thinking about putting their trust in God?"

Josh let out a heavy sigh. The prospect of losing this case wasn't something he wanted to picture.

Clare could sense the worry creeping onto Josh's face. "I'm not sure what will happen with the rest of this trial Mr. Randall," Clare said in a comforting voice. "But I am at peace with whatever the outcome."

Josh reflected upon her words. "Perhaps we are expecting too much. Maybe planting seeds is a lot like planting subliminal messages, one can never be quite certain if they will take root. I guess all we can do is pray for the best."

"See," said Clare optimistically. "How do you know that you haven't already given them all the necessary ingredients to point them in the right direction? I think that when people understand that there really is a loving God who wants to spend eternity with us, following Christ is the only logical path."

"I wish I could put my finger on it but it still feels as though there is something missing,"

Clare was not to be deterred. "In a perfect world we might be able to tie everything neatly together and put a cut little bow on it. However, you and I both know that if people are willing to seek out the truth, as they become more familiar with the Lord's Word, their faith will grow and the picture will start to come more clearly into focus."

Josh, sensing defeat, just nodded his head in agreement. "I guess we will just have to wait and see what tomorrow brings."

"That's the spirit," Adam said in his typical, chipper voice.

"I know this is a totally unrelated subject and I hope you don't think I am prying Mr. Randall, but what made you decide to go into criminal law?" Clare asked with genuine interest.

Josh paused for a moment, tilted his head slightly and asked... "Have you ever looked at someone and thought to yourself, there but for the grace of God go I?"

Clare nodded her head and said, "Of course."

"Well, when I was away at college one of my best friends growing up, died from a heroin overdose."

"I'm so sorry" Clare empathized, as she could see the sadness in his eyes.

"Me too," Josh sighed. "Such a terrible waste, but I know that could have easily been me."

Both Clare and Adam looked at each other and then back at Josh in astonishment.

"For those who knew me when I was younger, I was probably as far from being a Christian as humanly possible. I grew up acting like life was one giant party. Looking back on it, I think God was probably trying to get my attention all along. Although it may not have been intentional, I did my best to drown out His Voice. I suspect it is probably just human nature. God is speaking nothing but truth and sometimes the truth is hard to hear. It took a lot of pain before I finally decided to acknowledge Him. I'll spare you all the sordid details, but let's just say that once I finally came to my senses, I resolved to myself to try and make a difference. There is an old Hebrew saying - Your life is God's gift to you, what you choose to do with it, is your gift to God."

For some unknown reason, at that moment, Clare felt inexplicably drawn to him.

Josh thought about it for a second and then added, "I can't say with absolute certainty that I know that this is exactly what I am supposed to be doing with my time here on this planet, but maybe if I could inspire even one single person to ultimately change directions, I will have done something worthwhile with my life."

"I think I owe you an apology Mr. Randall," Clare blurted out.

Josh tilted his head a bit, "Why's that?"

"When we first met, I formed an opinion of you and I'm ashamed to say it wasn't very flattering." Clare confessed.

Josh shook his head ever so slightly and smiled to himself. "If anybody should be apologizing, it should be me. I like to test people. Sometimes I push the envelope too far. I probably shouldn't have expended so much energy trying to get under your skin."

Clare replayed their beginning conversations in her mind and all she could do was smile.

"Oh, one more thing Mr. Randall, I was wondering what ever happened to your nephew?"

"My nephew?" Josh repeated in a confused tone.

"The very first day when we came into your office you were talking to someone on the phone; I think his nickname might have been something like taco," Clare surmised.

"Ah" Josh smiled. "It's unethical for me to talk about other clients, but I'd like to think he's going to make it."

"I hope so, Mr. Randall." Clare said, as she gave him a hug goodbye.

"We might be a few minutes late tomorrow," Clare added, "but we should definitely be there before 9 am. I hope you have a wonderful evening and we shall see you in the morning."

"Take care," Josh said, smiling to his new friends.

the eleventh hour

Monday morning arrived as usual, and when Adam and Clare joined their attorney at their seats behind the defendant's table, they immediately noticed the absence of both Thomas and his partner Ethan. When the judge finally arrived and took his seat, the attorney for the plaintiff rose slightly and asked for permission to approach the bench.

"What's going on?" Clare whispered to Josh.

"I'm not sure," Josh replied, in a hushed tone.

After an animated conversation with lots of hand gestures, Jeremy Mendoza walked back to his table looking rather satisfied.

"Ladies and gentlemen of the jury," Judge Hayden announced, "unfortunately last night, the plaintiff, Mr. Addicott, was rushed to St. Anthony's Hospital with severe heart trauma. Although it is not customary, at this point I am granting the plaintiffs a temporary continuance. We will reconvene back here on Monday the 21st of June. As I am certain you are well aware, the same guidelines are in force, so please refrain from discussing this case with anyone and I realize that this may be an inconvenience but for the time being, please avoid all forms of social media. This court is adjourned."

let your light shine

Thomas heard a delicate knock, looked up and was surprised to see the defendants standing in the doorway of his hospital room. "What are you guys doing here?"

"Is it okay?" Adam asked with uncertainty.

Thomas gave them a nod and they came over to his bedside.

"How are you feeling?" Clare inquired.

"The doctor said it was just a mild heart attack and with a few days rest I should be fine."

"I'm very happy to hear that," Adam replied. "We just wanted to drop by with a present. Sort of a peace offering," and he gently placed a square, cardboard box on the bed next to Thomas.

"What's this?"

"Go ahead," said Adam, "it's for you."

"And your partner," Clare offered up with a gracious smile.

With that, Thomas slowly pulled the dangling end of the bow knot and released the string that was neatly tied around the box. When Thomas opened the flap, he was practically moved to tears. Inside was a beautifully decorated, miniature wedding cake with two identical figurines holding hands atop.

"Do you like it?" Clare asked with all sincerity.

"It's lovely," Thomas said, as he choked back the tears. "But after all that has happened, why are you being so nice to me?"

"In the grand scheme of things, what happens with this court case is inconsequential. When we heard that you were in the hospital," Adam volunteered, "it really scared us."

"It scared me too," Thomas confided. "But why the change of heart?"

"Let's just say," Clare admitted, "that I had an epiphany of sorts. I was wrong, not about my beliefs, but my actions. Please don't misunderstand what I am trying to say. We are in no way, trying to imply that we condone sin. Adam and I thought that by refusing to bake a wedding cake, we were defending God's Word.

I imagine, however, that from where you were sitting it must have felt an awful lot like we were judging you."

Thomas nodded his head in agreement.

"We are truly sorry for that," Adam acknowledged and then added, "we sincerely hope that you accept our apologies."

Thomas gave a slight nod and smiled.

"I suspect that there are probably some people who might consider my actions heresy;" Clare conceded, "but to my Christian brothers and sisters I would like to point out... You can't have it both ways. How can you possibly claim to believe in Christ and His teachings and at the same time be so focused upon denouncing sin that you are unwilling to help others understand the truth? Are you honestly that selfish, or do you have some sort of hidden agenda? Unless you are just pretending to be a Christian, I can't think of any other reason why you wouldn't want the people that you love to know that the way we get to spend eternity with God is simply by accepting that Jesus is God's Son and He paid the price in full for all our sins when He died on the cross."

"However," Clare confessed, "I've also come to the conclusion, that it is not my job to force you to subscribe to the exact same beliefs that I do. I understand that this is your life, and I have no right to demand that you live it a certain way. As Christians, we are simply called to love one another. Nothing more, nothing less. Who knows ... perhaps in time, some of that love may rub off and you might end up deciding for yourself that you want to search for the truth."

"I realize that you may find this hard to believe," Clare insisted, as she reached out and gently cradled his hand. "But my husband and I really do care about you. Hopefully this won't happen for a very, very long time, but ultimately one day you are going to die and I know that Heaven would be a much nicer place with you there."

Clare gave Thomas a few seconds to ponder on that last statement and then continued. "Here's a little secret... God wants to have a personal relationship with each and every one of us and we are all capable of hearing His Voice if we only take the time to really listen. Although it may feel a bit one-sided at the moment, are you seriously going to try and pretend that you are not part of this conversation?"

"Once you are truly willing to open your eyes, the evidence of God's handiwork is all around you. From the complexity of individual strands of DNA that dictate the genetic make-up of all living beings right up to the gravitational forces that control how planets, stars and galaxies interact. If you are being completely honest with yourself, you have to acknowledge that there is overwhelming evidence of intelligent design behind the creation of the universe."

"No one can force you to want to be with God, yet I truly hope you take the time to reconsider your thoughts as to where you would like to spend eternity. I am one hundred percent certain that once you examine all the evidence, and you finally come to the logical conclusion that GOD DOES EXIST: it really does become **a simple choice**."

Thomas smiled, but it was the added wink at the end that caught Clare off guard.

"God only knows, Mrs. Robinson, God only knows."

AUTHOR'S NOTE

Thank you for taking the time to read this book. I imagine that for some, this may have been a painful endeavor. As you probably already know, this wasn't meant to be some sort of literary masterpiece with an academy award-winning story. You were asked to read these words because I wanted you to understand in no uncertain terms that there is a God and He truly does love you.

It was also my hope that at some point it might actually occur to you that the plot and the characters are completely irrelevant. The entire purpose behind this book is to help give you (the reader) a better understanding of why Christianity is the truth. I realize that I am probably repeating myself, but this is extremely important. It is an absolute certainty that everyone reading these words will eventually die. This is a fact you cannot change.

Being a good person is not enough. You are deceiving yourself if you believe that everyone who dies will automatically go to heaven. If this were the case, then the choices we make in this lifetime would be of no consequence. All beliefs would therefore be completely equal. Despite what you may choose to think... THEY ARE NOT.

Sometimes one of the hardest things we can do in this world, is to try and share the truth with those whom we love. Anytime you bring up the subject of God, you run the risk of alienating people. It is quite possible that you may be so offended, that you will never want to speak to me again. I certainly hope that this isn't the case. I wanted you to read this because I sincerely do care about you, and I know that Heaven would be a much more colorful place with you there.

It is also conceivable that you may think I am delusional or that I have gone off the deep end with my beliefs. You might even be tempted to ask yourself...who am I to be so arrogant as to think that I have everything all figured out? Quite honestly, it is a valid question. The truth is: I don't have all the answers. My goal was simply to try and help nudge you in the right direction. If you are wondering how I can be so sure about my beliefs, the answer is amazingly simple - Ask Me!

Anyone who knows me well, understands that I am a deeply flawed human being. I had to make a mess of my life before God finally was able to get my attention. By all accounts, I am probably the least likely person God could have chosen to entice others to follow Jesus. My writing skills are practically nonexistent. I have no formal religious training, and most of my life I had absolutely no use for God. To be perfectly honest, the way I was living my life, I should have been dead a long time ago. I started drinking and doing drugs at age eleven. My morals, or lack thereof, were questionable at best. Sadly, a great percentage of my time here on this planet would have been considered extremely offensive to God.

I would like to be able to blame drugs and alcohol for my inexcusable and disgusting behavior but in the end, the choices were all mine. I am deeply ashamed of many of my actions. I am so sorry for all the pain I have caused. For those I have hurt and betrayed, my only hope is that one day you can find it in your heart to forgive me. There is a great biblical passage that I think will succinctly sum up much of my life.

"Here is a trustworthy saying that deserves full acceptance: Christ Jesus came into the world to save sinners—of whom I am the worst. But for that very reason I was shown mercy so that in me, the worst of sinners, Christ Jesus might display his immense patience as an example for those who would believe in him and receive eternal life." (1 Timothy 1: 15-16)

Please don't be misconstrued, do not let my shortcomings keep you from seeking the truth. I am begging you, regardless of what you may think of me, please do not be so stubborn that you refuse to do your own research.

Unfortunately, we are all flawed human beings. However, once we announce that we are Christians, our flaws seem to become magnified for the world to see. Whenever we fail to act in a Christ-like manner, our hypocrisy sticks out like a sore thumb and this is what most people immediately notice. Sadly, this causes many people to question the validity of Christ. Just because there are far too many Christians that give Christianity a bad name, does not mean you should toss the baby out with the bathwater.

Think about it this way, if there really was an all-powerful God (A Heavenly Father) who loves us unconditionally, and He had a Son who came to earth ... how would He act? What would He try to teach us? The more you examine the life of Jesus, the more you will come to realize that there is no possible way His wisdom could have come from this world. He is so much more than just a good teacher with ideas that were way ahead of His time.

I am confident that if you are willing to take the time to really examine Jesus' life and learn about what He was teaching, I believe that there is only one possible conclusion you can reach. You will see that Jesus is neither a liar, nor a lunatic and He, therefore, must be telling the truth. However, none of this will make sense unless you have a desire to know the truth and in order to know the truth, you must take the time to read God's Word.

If you are still reluctant to conduct your own investigation, ask yourself – WHY? There has to be some underlying reason. Considering yourself to be spiritual but not religious, is not going to help you come any closer to understanding the truth. Kind of thinking that there might possibly be some sort of a God, may be a good first step, but it is definitely not the same thing as putting your faith and complete trust in Him.

Most people are not afraid to have an in-depth conversation with their dog or cat, but they are somehow reluctant to talk to God. Even if you still have lingering doubts, you can actually ask Him for His help. There are no magic words to recite, you could simply say something like... "God, I'm not even certain if you exist, but if you do, please help me understand the TRUTH." God made a promise to the world, that He would make Himself available to all who seek Him in earnest.

It is perfectly normal to be skeptical. It is possible that some people may even rationalize that if there really was an All-Powerful God, He could easily make Himself known to me if He wanted to. Why wouldn't He simply communicate directly? The truth is, He already has.

What if God has the power to use the written word to speak directly to you? What if God actually gave us a book to help us understand Him? There is a great little acronym that comes to mind. **B.I.B.L.E.**

Basic **I**nstructions **B**efore Leaving **E**arth. The more you read, the more you will come to understand that it is not merely empty words on a page, but it is actually God reaching out and communicating directly with you.

No one can force you pick up a bible and start reading, but if you were offered a job that paid several million dollars per year on the condition that you read the owner's manual: wouldn't you take the time to do so? Well, spending eternity with God is infinitely more important. Why would you want to leave something so valuable up to chance? Do you really want to ignore the truth and turn you back on God? Most of us are procrastinators by nature. We tend to put off things that we think will be painful or unpleasant. Despite what you might imagine, finding out that there is a God and that He loves you unconditionally isn't exactly terrible news, nor does it mean that your life will no longer be enjoyable. For those of you who are still on the fence: I beg of you, please don't make the fatal mistake of thinking that you have forever to make up your mind.

Since Jesus is an integral part of this story, I would suggest that you start by reading the New Testament. Consider it a quest for the truth. There are really only two possible choices... Either it is some sort of elaborate hoax or it is the truth. If you think that it is a hoax, you must ask yourself who are the beneficiaries? Certainly not Jesus, nor His Disciples. Even a great many of the early Christians were killed for their beliefs. It seems pretty far-fetched to believe that all these people willingly went to their deaths just to dupe a bunch of strangers some two thousand years in the future. Unfortunately, there are some people in this world who are so blinded by hatred that they will stop at nothing to prevent others from learning the truth.

"Whoever claims to love God and hates his brother is a liar. For whoever does not love their brother whom they have seen, cannot love God whom they have not seen."
1 John 4:20

It all circles back to **LOVE**.

"Love is patient and kind; love does not envy or boast; it is not arrogant or rude. It does not insist on its own way; it is not irritable or resentful; it does not rejoice at wrongdoing, but rejoices with the truth."
1 Corinthians 13: 4-6

"For God so loved the world that He gave His only begotten Son, that whoever believes in Him should not perish but have everlasting life."

John 3:16

I would like to leave you with this final thought. I want you to imagine a beautiful fountain that never runs dry. The difference, however, is that instead of plain, ordinary water, this fountain produces an endless supply of perfect, unconditional LOVE.

Think about the kind of love a parent has for a newborn...and multiply that by infinity.

Once again, I am not asking you to take my word for it, go and find out for yourself. I believe it can be best summed up in one neat little equation ... **GOD = LOVE**.

"And you shall know the truth and the truth shall set you free."

Epilogue

In order to make the story seem a bit more realistic, I have included a very limited amount of profanity. It is entirely conceivable that you may find this fact so disturbing that you would never want others to read it. Do you honestly believe that it is more important to pretend that you no longer sin and have achieved absolute perfection, rather than help someone understand the truth?

I am not arguing that we shouldn't strive to be better people, but being a better person isn't a prerequisite for salvation.

If you are troubled by the fact that this book makes no mention of certain doctrines, what you are implying to the world is that simply putting your trust in Jesus is not the answer. In essence, what you are literally saying is that people must accept EVERYTHING, from the very first day, EXACTLY the same way you see it.

Wouldn't it be much more prudent to help people comprehend the fundamentals first?

Have you ever stopped to consider that maybe we aren't meant to learn everything all at once? I happen to like math because numbers actually prove that there is intelligent design behind the creation of the universe. Math is orderly and rational. Can't you see that starting off by teaching someone the basics such as addition and subtraction, is not the same thing as arguing that calculus and trigonometry are wrong. Maybe learning is supposed to be a step by step process. Everyone needs to start at the beginning.

Understanding the truth is, by no means, a license to be intolerant or insensitive towards the views of others. People of all faiths are to be respected. It might make you feel good to think you are being inclusive by considering all beliefs to be equal; but the reality is that logic and reason dictate that this is impossible.

There can only be one truth, plain and simple. The time is coming to stand and be counted. I am aware that this may frustrate and anger some people but no one is being forced to accept this fact.

Regrettably, there will be some people who may be content to denounce Christianity in the pursuit of personal power, what's going to be your excuse? Just for the record, this book serves absolutely no purpose sitting on a shelf. It is meant to be read and passed along to someone you love.

CPSIA information can be obtained
at www.ICGtesting.com
Printed in the USA
FSHW020937230320
68374FS

9 781546 220367